*Penguin Books*
## ALEX IN WINT[ER]

The race is over and [Alex is certain]
that she will be selected to swim for New Zealand
at the 1960 Olympics in Rome. But is it a
certainty?

Life is complicated for Alex. She is finding it
difficult to adjust to the death of Andy, but is still
determined to beat her rival, Maggie. Anxiety
about selection and her irritation at being treated
like a child are almost too much for Alex. There
are times when it seems that winter will never end.

*Alex in Winter* is the award-winning sequel to *Alex*.
It is the second book in a trilogy.

# ALEX IN WINTER

Tessa Duder

PENGUIN BOOKS

## PENGUIN BOOKS

Penguin Books (NZ) Ltd, 182-190 Wairau Road, Auckland 10, New Zealand
Penguin Books Ltd, 27 Wrights Lane, London W8 5TZ, England
Penguin USA, 375 Hudson Street, New York, NY 10014, United States
Penguin Books Australia Ltd, 487 Maroondah Highway, Ringwood, Australia 3134
Penguin Books Canada Ltd, 10 Alcorn Avenue, Toronto, Ontario, Canada M4V 1E4

Penguin Books Ltd, Registered Offices: Harmondsworth, Middlesex, England

First published by Oxford University Press, 1989
Published in Penguin Books in 1991
1 3 5 7 9 10 8 6 4 2

Copyright © Tessa Duder, 1989
All rights reserved
The moral right of the author has been asserted

Offset from the Oxford University Press edition
Printed by Australian Print Group, Maryborough, Vic.

Except in the United States of America, this book is sold subject
to the condition that it shall not, by way of trade or otherwise, be
lent, re-sold, hired out or otherwise circulated without the publisher's
prior consent in any form of binding or cover other than that in which
it is published and without a similar condition including this condition
being imposed on the subsequent purchaser.

# Contents

Part One   vii
Part Two   41
Part Three   79
Part Four   139

# Part One

TO get from the floodlit water up on to the victory dais was not really a very great distance. It involved only the swimmer climbing from the shallow end of the pool, drying off, regaining some sort of normal breathing, blinking eyes into focus; waiting while the judges and timekeepers went into their huddles. A minute perhaps, or in this case nearly three, longer than the race itself. And then, as the announcer called the placings, two steps up on to the top level of the dais.

The new champion was seen to falter.

Hard-bitten journalists watching through binoculars from the Press box above the starting end thought they had an even better story about to break.

'What's wrong with the kid?'

'I've seen some burned out young in this game,' said a bald veteran of forty years' experience covering every sport known to his paper's readers, 'but . . . it was only a sprint, for Chrissake. Two laps!'

'She can't even get out of the pool.'

A silence fell in the Press box while the unplaced girls climbed out, leaving only Maggie and Alex, longer than was usual, while the crowd's clapping merged into an excited buzz. Alex groped for the side of the pool; lay across it like a stranded fish; tried once, fell back and tried again, taking her weight on her rigid arms, hanging suspended with her head down on her chest, until she'd gathered the strength to heave a knee up and crawl on to the side of the pool. She sat slumped on the edge with her eyes closed while an official in whites and blazer, concern in every curve of her motherly figure, squatted down beside her and slung a large towel and track suit top around her shoulders.

At her feet, Maggie eased her own quite different pain by swimming away, a few strokes of backstroke, filling her ears with water, shutting out the sight and sound of a standing ovation which she knew was not for her.

'Do they have a doctor at these shows?' said one of the reporters.

'Bound to be, somewhere in this crowd. Or the St John's

ambulance people. But she's standing, at least!'

'Women's 100 metres freestyle.' The announcer's voice abruptly silenced the three thousand people who had come to see this race and who — since they could not separate the two swimmers at the finish — had not been disappointed. He paused dramatically, spinning out the moment. On the Napier beach, a hundred yards away, Pacific waves crashed noisily on to the black and grey stones.

'First — the new New Zealand champion — from Auckland, Miss Alex Archer . . .'

The crowded stands and terraces exploded with cheers, applause, whistles and banners.

'She's not going to make it.'

'She's a zombie. Look at her face.'

'Oh, God,' said the veteran. 'I've had enough of watching kids kill themselves in the name of sport.' He put down his binoculars, took a long pull on the scraggy remains of a roll-your-own cigarette, and looked around the huge crowd now on its feet, still cheering and clapping. 'Blood sports, in effect. The Romans have a lot to answer for.'

The only woman reporter, herself once a sprint champion, as tall as Alex and ten years older, said, 'You're being melodramatic. She's all right.'

The veteran, thinking of his nine-year-old granddaughter who had just started training and who worshipped the ground Alex walked on, stubbed out his fag and reluctantly took up his binoculars. Alex had put on the bright blue track suit top, smoothed back her hair with the comb the official gave her, and slowly made it to the top step of the dais. She was standing erect, staring ahead. The image was close and clear enough to expose tears, a gaunt face drained of colour, eyesockets deep in shadow, the pulse beating fast in the side of her neck, and chest still heaving. Photographers' flash bulbs went off below, but she gave no sign of having noticed, even less of smiling for the camera.

'Bill Jack's not very happy,' said the veteran swinging his glasses on to the trio of Alex's coach, father and grandmother, whose anxious expressions contrasted sharply with the smiling faces and clapping hands on all sides. 'There's something funny going on with that kid. If I were her parents I'd be worried.'

'Time, a new national record, sixty-four point nine,' boomed the announcer, unable to keep the delight out of his voice. As the cheers and applause again rose into the soft February night air, the face in the circular image of the glasses was seen to smile slightly.

'She earned that,' said the woman reporter.

'What's that she's fastening round her neck?' said another.

'Some sort of gold chain, a pearl, I think.' Probably very special in some way, but she wasn't going to tell her cynical male colleagues that.

'A bauble.' This younger reporter put down his binoculars, disappointed that Alex was controlling whatever turmoil was going on inside. It looked like the hoped for front page human-interest story (a faint, breakdown, stretcher case perhaps) wasn't going to eventuate. He leaned forward, smirking slightly as he peered through the glasses. 'Fine pair o' legs! If I was in the business of advertising stockings, I'd grab those legs. Figuratively speaking, of course.'

'Would you now.' The woman reporter looked sideways, not relishing the thought of future evenings spent sitting in Press boxes with this slimy newcomer, with his loud tie and over-oiled hair. 'Exploitation, the old story.'

'Rubbish. Women love it, the implied promise, if you wear our nylons you too can have legs like that. That girl could get a job as a swim-suit model tomorrow.'

'For your information, Ross, Alex is a schoolgirl and an amateur and bound to the amateur code. And she's got better things to do with her life than advertise nylons or swim-suits.'

'But you have to admit it's a spectacular body. Now Maggie there, neat enough little figure, bit muscular in the calves perhaps, too flat in the chest. Doesn't hold a candle.'

'She. A young woman, not a body.'

'Oh, come on . . .'

'Second,' interrupted the announcer, 'the previous title-holder, Miss Maggie Benton, in a time of sixty-five seconds.'

'A tenth of a second! Well, I certainly couldn't separate them,' said the veteran, his fingers carefully rolling another cigarette from shreds of tobacco and a leaf of thin paper. 'We might see a protest from the mother. She's not looking too pleased over there.'

'Naa, it was clear enough.' The implication of better eyesight did not escape the veteran, catching the woman reporter's amused glance. Ross went on, unperturbed, 'Now isn't *that* a touching sight.'

To those still watching closely, Alex's eyes were seen to have flown open at the mention of Maggie's name. She was looking down, extending a hand and stepping down to the lower level as the two came together and hugged closely. It was clearly spontaneous, not set up for the photographers whose flash bulbs caught the moment. The woman reporter said sharply, 'You're new to this game, Ross. You don't know what those two have been through, for years. They're actually good friends.'

'I don't believe it.'

'It's a fact. And if you think Alex looks a bit overwrought, she's had a rough spin these last few months, apart from what happened last night. I didn't rate her chances of winning very highly. Perhaps you should also know that she had something going for a lad who was killed in a hit-and-run road accident, about nine weeks ago. Bowled off his bike by a drunkard. She used to train with him.'

'Really?' said Ross. The woman caught the interest in his voice.

'Off limits, Ross. Alex won't tell you anything on that score. You'll leave it strictly alone if you know what's good for you.'

Ross did know, from deliberately upsetting Alex just before the heats that morning, telling her in the calculated hope of an angry quote to catch his midday deadline, that she was under threat of being suspended and disqualified from competing. She had told him to go away, two polite words of profound contempt. He had admired her control, for a kid.

The third placegetter had climbed on to the dais. The crowd, knowing the ritual, was silent for the fanfare being played by two young trumpeters from the town band, but burst forth again in prolonged clapping while the three girls were handed their medals by the local mayor.

'I'd pick both of them for Rome,' said the veteran. 'Maggie is sane enough, nice uncomplicated sort of kid, as long as her mother stays out of the picture. But our Alex there . . .' He thought he'd seen it all: bright kids in high-pressure sports, swimming, athletics, gymnastics, tennis, in football and rowing teams; kids shoved forward by pushy parents, fired up by ambitious coaches, manipulated by empire-building, mealy-minded officials; twelve-year-old puppets, specializing too soon, pushed too hard, bored and burned out before they even left school.

Hadn't he seen it all time and time again, and growing worse in recent years? Shaking his head now, watching closely as the three girls came off the dais, Alex last, still moving slowly, too slowly — he wasn't so sure. Bill Jack, he noted, had taken the unusual step of forcing his way on to the crowded concourse to lead her away from the engulfing press of photographers, officials, young swimmers, and applause which had broken out yet again, louder and longer than he had heard around a swimming pool in years.

---

I just won the race of my life.

Overcoming a battle to the death with officials and a certain mother, no sleep, my period a week early, two false starts, hitting the lane ropes and a disastrous turn, I still did it!

At the finish the world went into weird slow motion. (Strange, did nobody else notice?) I suppose I stood on the victory dais with the gold medal in my hands while the trumpets played. I think I was crying, I can't really remember getting up or getting down. Mr Jack was somewhere around. Then I vaguely remember being congratulated and hugged by the most unlikely people and interviewed for the papers and the radio. God only knows what I said, 'cause I don't. I was photographed, but I remember now, I insisted only with Maggie because the result could have gone either way and she was still smiling, admittedly a bit wan, but that's more than I could say for her mother. I rang home and heard my Mum actually weeping and the brats cheering at the other end of the phone. Dad and Gran were over the moon, crying too.

I am more than likely to be nominated for the Olympics in Rome, six months away.

So why can't I sleep? Why, hearing a town clock strike one, am I once again lying on this lumpy motel bed listening to my room-mate snore? And why am I sweating from a nightmare, just as bad as last night's which drove me to a midnight swim and nearly got me disqualified from the sprint and any chance of Rome altogether. Isn't it all over, this crazy yearning?

And the dreams! There are two versions, but always the same components: Andy, me, his yacht and more wind than we can handle. In one version we are sailing perilously along, but laughing and singing, thrilling to the speed. There's a gust which lays us on our ear. Andy is caught off balance, falls overboard, The boat recovers, I sail on. He doesn't come up. The water turns a sinister streaky dusky brown.

If that isn't bad enough, the second is worse: this time the boat does capsize, in slow motion. This time it's me that goes, deep deeply under, tangled with ropes and sails and wires that grow tighter around my neck my arms my chest and that's when I wake up sweating, gasping, telling my room-mate that it's nothing, sorry I yelled, woke you up, go back to sleep. I don't want to remember any more, please God, no. Andy was run down by a car, two months ago. I went to his funeral, and saw that awful long box being carried past me. I saw the dent on his bed where he'd had a nap a few hours before he got mashed up. I spent part of Christmas day with his parents. I have trained myself into the ground for him. I won tonight's race for him. It's over.

There's something else bugging me.

After all the final relays and victory ceremonies and speeches were done, I'd stood holding court at the cup-of-tea-and-sausage-roll party for officials and senior swimmers held in the clubrooms above the pool. It wasn't intentional; I was literally pinned into a corner by officials who were old friends, several reporters, other swimmers, all wanting to talk or get me to sign programmes or autograph books. Over their head I could see Mr Jack with a group of coaches, Dad and Gran talking to Maggie with a few officials. I was glad they were talking to her; they knew as well as anyone how she was feeling, being pipped at the post. They'd had a lot of practice with me, over the years.

I was relieved when Dad suggested that Gran was a bit tired and was I ready to leave? I knew there was a group of swimmers planning to go to a milk bar, maybe walk along the beach and stay up until dawn, to unwind after our months of hard training, but that wasn't for me, tonight. My victory smile was already wearing thin.

'Yes, I'm ready,' I said, but beside my elbow a very patient young male reporter from the local paper wanted a few minutes, Miss Archer? Somewhere quiet, he said, politer and more earnest than any reporter I'd ever met. Tomorrow morning, I suggested, but he was sorry he had another assignment tomorrow morning and afternoon was no good as I'd be on my way back to Auckland. Would I mind, only a few minutes? So we went along the passage, to a sort of alcove. All the lights were still on. It was after about ten minutes, during a long silence while he was busy trying to remember his shorthand and I was busy trying to stay awake, that I heard the voices coming along the corridor.

'Here's the committee room. Pity about the sprint title.'

'Indeed, Albie, a great pity. Ten yards out, even five, I thought young Maggie had the race sewn up. Great shame for the kid. It's made the nominations difficult.'

With the huge crowd gone from the spectator stands, the officials and swimmers' party thinning out, and the reporters off to drink at a hotel with a friendly and not particularly law-abiding publican, the selectors could be forgiven for thinking they had the place to themselves.

Not that stocky Albie Jones would have noticed a stray competitor anyway. Half a lifetime as a primary school headmaster and swimming official had made him impervious to children, except inside schoolgrounds in controllable lines. Swimmers he saw only as meticulous entries in his personal register of local and international times.

'As title-holder Alex must now have the prior claim,' said Cyril Upjohn, his official's blazer straining across a pigeon chest and a well-padded backside. He paused outside the door that was being held open for him, and poked a match down into the bowl of his pipe, before continuing.

'I can't say I like the girl, really. Too much to say for herself, too inclined to argue, a bad influence on juniors. I dislike tall women, even young ones. I don't want her in Rome.'

'Well, as the likely manager, Cyril,' said the miniature headmaster, also immaculate in whites and a blazer, 'you'll have to cope with her. Maggie, not Alex, and young Brett David was how I'd seen it.'

'Could be.'

'Not,' said Albie Jones, flipping open his precious file, 'not that either of them would make an Olympic final, on current times. We'll be lucky to see a swimmer in the team.'

'I think, Albie, we'll have to announce a delay. If Maggie can get that record down, substantially down, she'd be back as first choice. Ah, here's Brian, come in, come in. We were just discussing, postponement, do you think?'

A third elderly man in blazer and white trousers had been guided to the committee room by the resonant voices of men who were well used to making themselves heard. The door was closed. Half an hour, two pipes, an ashtray of cigarettes and six double whiskies later, they had formally confirmed the postponement that Cyril Upjohn had proposed in the first place. They drafted a brief Press statement, carefully, because this wasn't the end of their responsibilities, for release in Monday's papers, and returned to their hotel rather tired. If only that wretched girl hadn't pulled off a major surprise, (or, thought Cyril Upjohn, she'd managed to get herself properly disqualified last night), things would have been so much simpler and tidier.

---

The wrong place, the wrong time. And the wrong script, the wrong words.

Even when the door closed, I could still hear the ringing tones of my least favourite official and that small headmaster called Albie Jones, who minced around holding forth to anyone who would listen about times which had been done at the last European championships by obscure Hungarians.

'I've heard enough,' I whispered to the fascinated boy beside me. I took my sandals off and tiptoed as silently as I knew how down the echoing corridor and three flights of stairs. They might hear us, but once they'd climbed to their geriatric feet and opened the door, they'd never see or catch us or prove anything.

'You'd be wise to keep that to yourself,' I said, outside the pool's main entrance. My sixteen-year-old friend (who I noted had also taken his black shoes off) was panting and flushed, wondering how he could use this juicy bit of information. A scoop?! And also embarrassed for me, I think. It's not every day you get to hear home truths about what top officials think of their swimmers, and one in particular.

'Sounds as though you don't have many friends in high places, Miss Archer.'

'I don't. No that's not true. It's only Mr Upjohn who's got it in for me. But don't try anything clever. They'll get you, write to your editor, withdraw your Press pass, silence you somehow. Like they nearly got me.'

He probably knew; it had got around, rumours about Alex running round the town with a married man the night before the final. As if I'd be so *stupid!* I'd nearly not been allowed to swim in the final; I had been officially reprimanded for taking a midnight swim, which I needed to stop me going off my rocker on the night in question. They would like to have believed Mrs Benton's tittle-tattle version, pure invention. Then I could have been suspended and Maggie could have won easily and been nominated for Rome, and everyone would have been happy.

'I could write the story, informed sources say . . .'

'Please, forget it,' I said from the superior wisdom of my six seasons in swimming. 'They'll deny everything. You'll achieve nothing, except more trouble for me.'

'But you'd think they didn't *want* any swimmers . . .'

'Funny, I had that impression too.' He was flipping back through the pages of his shorthand. 'Can you read that stuff?' I asked.

'Sort of,' he said, blushing. 'I've only been learning for a month. Is that true, you wouldn't get into the Olympic final?'

'Who knows? Dawn Fraser's world record is sixty point something, there are lots around the sixty-three mark. Who can say what we might do, Maggie or me, or anyone, with the sort of competition people in Aussie, or England, or America, or Europe get all the time.' As usual, I was talking myself into a state. 'I'd better be going.'

'Can I use that as a quote?'

'Yes, you can say that it's amazing that New Zealand swimmers do as well as they do, *all* things considered.'

'Lack of competition . . .'

'Lack of competition, official encouragement, training facilities, anything you like, make it up, that's what most reporters do. No, except what we just heard up there, that's for real, that's . . . oh *hell*.' I was losing control. Even under the street lights I could see he was hurt. I had to trust this boy.

'Sorry, I didn't mean — what's your name?'

'Grant Davies.'

'Grant, look, I have to go. Please, don't drop me in it.'

'Thanks for your time, Miss Archer. And good luck . . . with the nominations.'

'Thanks. Hope you've got enough.' He didn't deserve my scorn. He'd asked some quite intelligent questions, for a reporter, like what did I, a true amateur, think of the Australian and Communist countries' training camps which many people thought were a violation of the amateur code (envious, I said), and how much did my parents contribute to my success? Everything, I said; my parents, my little old grandmother who was born right here in Napier you know, even my brothers and little sister, they all did.

I went over to meet up with Mr Jack, Dad and the said little old Gran sitting on the edge of a raised flower bed, waiting for me. Outwardly the champ, a woman of the world. Inside I am seething, confused, sick at heart as we walk silently along the Marine Parade back to the hotel. The breakers crash on the nearby beach. It seems like twenty-four days, not twenty-four hours, since I sat on the beach last night and contemplated finishing it all. I have dreamed of this victory for months, longed for the security of the nomination in my pocket, my rightful due, the satisfaction of lining up for the next hurdle.

I've done it — and — nothing. Nothing.

Why is it always *me* — taking pity on a polite but insistent cub reporter in a tie and walk-shorts, giving him time and co-operation. If I'd been Maggie, say, my Dad would have said enough, no more, and taken me home to bed. And then I'd never have been sitting in that alcove behind a potted plant with my ears burning, when I should have been drinking tea quietly back at the hotel, enjoying my win, thinking of the amazing trip to Rome I'd just earned.

'I don't want her in Rome,' he said.

Andy, you have betrayed me.

On the long drive back to Auckland the next day they put my unusual quietness down to nervous exhaustion, the understandable anticlimax. Sunday night Mum had planned a celebration dinner, with Mr Jack and his wife as honoured guests. Sweet local bubbly, roast pork with crispy golden crackling and apple sauce, Mum's most magnificent pavlova, as big as a road sign. Excitable kids, Mr Jack at his jovial best, his wife plump and happy, Gran all fired up after her trip down memory lane to the town where she'd spent most of her life, and frequent phone calls of congratulations all meant I did not have to contribute much to the party. I smiled weakly at the toasts, and said thank you to the telephone callers and tried not to weep and to forget all the rest.

Dad woke me next morning from a groggy sleep with a cup of tea and the newspaper. 'School today.'

Through gummed-up eyes I saw the sports page, with a large picture of me and Maggie on the victory dais, taken from below to distort the length of our legs. A chorus girl, the sort of photo I'd got very cunning at avoiding, but not this time. Maggie, a head shorter, smiling manfully.

'Nice picture.'

'*Dad!* It's awful. Glamour puss stuff.'

'Sleep well?'

'Not particularly.' I scanned the report, which said some nice things about the superb duel we had fought, my fighting spirit in victory and Maggie's sporting spirit in defeat and how both of us should be nominated for Rome.

'Look below,' Dad said quietly. 'I'm sorry, you won't be pleased.'

And there, sure enough, was a small story that the National Selectors, Messrs C. D. S. Upjohn, A. R. V. Jones, and B. J. Webster, had announced that the Olympic nominations would be held open for six weeks until the middle of March, to give 'the small vein of candidates' a chance to improve their times. The general impression was that not one of us was good enough.

I heard Mum's voice from the doorway, unusually holding forth. 'No encouragement, no indication of possible candidates, no times to aim at, nothing. It's a disgrace. I sometimes wonder if these men ever stop to think what it means to youngsters who train five miles a day, who give their waking hours to their sport. And their families and coaches. They don't do it for a slap in the face.'

When I said nothing, but just went on staring at the paper, Dad said, 'Alex?'

'What?'

'Did you know about this? Did Mr Jack hear something?'

Was I that transparent? Gran had now arrived in her dressing gown; a third tired unsmiling face. 'Why do you say that?'

'You just don't seem surprised.'

'I'm not, are you? We've never actually been told, except for some vague notion about times good enough to get into an Olympic final. How can they know that, from four years ago, records falling all the time? It's guesswork. Sixty-four point nine, never mind a record, still three seconds behind Dawn Fraser. And two nominations for one stroke? Of course I knew.'

'Unconvincing,' said Mum, who'd given me a close once-over as she came to collect my dirty clothes for washing and had no doubt seen the pain in my eyes. 'Don't tell me . . .'

'Mum, leave it out.'

Gran, now sitting on my bed and rubbing my arm sympathetically, interrupted. 'Don't upset her, Helena. Naturally she's disappointed, aren't we all? Of course she'll get nominated. How could she not? She's the champion. It's only the others they're not sure about.'

Dear Gran, so sure and optimistic, and Mum so upset on my behalf, and Dad too, and now James and Debbie going on about it not being fair, and my cheesecakey picture grinning at me out of the morning paper, applauded and rejected on the same page. I can't tell you why I am screaming inside. It's worse than you will ever know.

---

'Alex, would you come forward please?'

Miss Constantia Gillies looked over the lectern, over the heads of seven hundred girls, towards the back of the crowded school hall. Morning assemblies compelled her, as principal, to face this spectacle daily. The uniform was dreary enough: white blouse and short socks, above-knee gym tunic belted around the middle (in summer, a dull blue, in winter, black; unflattering and demeaning, and the all-male Board of Governors resistant to any suggestion of change), black regulation shoes. Worse was the regulation short hairstyle, not touching the collar; most disturbing was the regulation expression, incurious and slightly hostile. Every morning she wondered about the effect of such clothes on young minds and spirits.

'Alex?' called Miss Gillies, putting her spectacles back on. Pupils thought this taking on and off was a spinsterish habit; a few staff knew it was her defence when the sight of massed girls became unbearably depressing.

She believed Alex had arrived at school today, a week late from the long summer holidays because of her triumphs at the national swimming championships. The school, already restless in the heat and sensing an interesting hitch, was shuffling. Eventually, a head with fairish hair cut unusually short could be seen above the others, moving slowly from the back. As Alex neared the steps leading up on to the stage, Miss Gillies began to regret her decision to call the child forward. A mention would have been enough.

'I agree, it was a mistake,' she said afterwards in the staff room to an angry drama teacher. 'But we hadn't seen her for over two months. How could we have known?'

'What she needs is less adulation, not more,' said Marcia Macrae, who had also watched Alex's progress towards the stage with mounting alarm. The sluggish walk, the sullen eyes, the atypical ungraciousness — all indicated anger and depression, either unresolved or caused by some new problem. She was not even bothering to hide her pain; this girl who had as much talent as any Marcia Macrae had ever taught. She was verging on thin rather than slender. She looked nearer twenty-five than fifteen.

'One must expect,' said Miss Gillies, 'some sort of reaction.'

'Naturally,' said Marcia Macrae with scorn. 'Reaction to success, sleepless nights, to pressure from all sides. To a grief as profound as any I've seen and only two months along its course. She needs very careful handling. Reinforcement of her social role, understanding of her anger and loneliness. Recognition that a girlfriend ostensibly outside the family can grieve as deeply as someone inside it. Encouragement to think about something else other than swimming.'

Miss Gillies sighed. 'What are her after-school activities this year?'

'Swimming, swimming and swimming. Oh yes, calisthenics, weights. From what I gather, reading this morning's paper, a probable trip to Rome in August, more pressure.'

'What about her ballet, piano?'

'Quit, as far as I know, more's the pity.'

'Well, there's no doubt about her accrediting prospects, provided she keeps up with the homework. Even allowing for two months away in August and September. Her School Certificate results were quite remarkable, all things considered. We can keep her on the fringes of choir, the musical production, any plays you might be planning, Marcia?'

Miss Macrae busied herself collecting up books for the next class, avoiding a direct answer. She had every intention of involving Alex in *something* during the second term, and on her return from Rome, if only as an antidote to all that training. Alex's gifts were too unusual to be watered down by her current mania for punishing herself in a pool.

'I'll talk to the parents,' said Miss Gillies, unfolding her long bird-like limbs to their full six foot two inches. She was always glad when the first two weeks of the school year were over, and staff and school had settled down to regular work. Depressed pupils were more commonly a problem in the winter term, or as exams approached. Around the large staff room, women in black gowns drained their coffee cups and responded to a loud bell signalling the end of break.

'Anything to keep that girl on an even keel,' said Miss Macrae bluntly. 'Frankly, she disturbs me.'

---

I had two days off training to settle down at school, 'before we have a final crack at that record, Alex?' Perhaps Mr Jack anticipated how awful school was going to be: torture, with gushing teachers and moony juniors hanging round the cloakrooms asking for autographs, wanting to carry my bags.

Then there was Miss Gillies hauling me up on the stage at

Monday assembly. I very nearly refused to go up; in the end, prodded on all sides by the people around me, I couldn't care if I went or not. I had to stand there, while La Constantia went on about courage and stuff and then presented me with two books, 'By Katherine Mansfield and Vera Brittain, strong, interesting women, both.' Dutiful applause. Yawn.

Julia, my wheezy and scientific friend, was harder to fool. She'd been away that morning at the dentist, but at lunchtime, when I thought I'd have some time to myself under the far trees of the playing field, she found me, and didn't waste any time considering we hadn't seen each other since Christmas.

'What's happened to your nomination? What was all that stuff in the paper about delaying the nominations until next month.'

'I don't know. I'll just have to do better, won't I.'

'Don't they tell you *anything*?'

'We read about it in the papers like anyone else.'

She waited but I know the interviewer's trick of silence, waiting for you to break and say what you meant not to say.

'That's rough,' she said, eventually.

I shrugged. So she went off on a tangent, talking about the special nursing home for unmarried mothers she'd visited during the holidays. Not the most cheering topic of conversation.

'Remember Jackie?'

I did — Jackie in our class who in the middle of last year had put on rather a lot of weight and vanished. Dark rumours told of a baby boy, adopted out, and her now working in a bank in town and, according to those who'd seen her, looking defeated and sad and ten years older than sixteen.

'I read about this place in a magazine, with discreet photos so you couldn't see the faces. Jackie had her baby there. One of mum's friends, her husband is a visiting doctor. So I got in touch and asked him to show me around. I told him not to tell Mum, of course.'

'Of course.'

'He was quite encouraging about me wanting to be an obstetrician, in a patronizing sort of way. When I asked if I could watch a birth, that was another matter. "Plenty of time for that, young lady, during your training . . ." — went all stuffy and pompous, you know.'

'Yeah.'

She struggled on, her voice showing all the familiar signs of an imminent asthma attack. 'There was something creepy — all those huge dumpy girls. Twenty or thirty of them sitting around knitting bootees and matinee jackets. Pink for a girl, blue for a boy. Waiting for babies they're not allowed to keep.'

'Who says?'

'The doc' says. All the babies get adopted. There are plenty of people waiting, he said, specially for cute little baby girls.'

'Where're the fathers in all this?'

'Not even mentioned. They escaped, didn't they. Well, I suppose if you're lucky, you have parents who insist on a shotgun wedding, get you married off good and quick.'

'That's not luck, that's press-gang. No one's going to marry me off,' I said fiercely. 'I'm never going to get married, ever. As for babies . . .'

'You'll meet someone . . .'

'*Else*? You sound like my mother. No I won't.'

'What's the matter, Alex? You look awful. It's not just Andy. It can't be just the delay in the nominations.'

'*Just* Andy, isn't that enough?'

'I didn't mean it like that,' she said wearily, yet determined to prod me further. 'But you beat Maggie and you're going to Rome, what more do you want for heaven's sake, and you can't stay angry for ever.'

'Don't bet on it, and I won't be going to Rome, not if . . .' She had nearly succeeded! 'I'm just tired, all right? Dad's going on about feeling a bit flat after reaching the heights, etcetera, etcetera. Beware of the day you get your heart's desire.'

'If it's the trip to Rome, you haven't actually got it yet,' she said pointedly. 'When does the final Games team get picked?'

'May.'

'So, it doesn't apply. But there's something . . .'

'There's nothing.' I stood up, screwing the remains of my uneaten lunch into a tight ball and throwing it under the hedge. I saw surprise in Julia's eyes. 'I've got some stationery to get from the office.'

And there was the pill bottle, being unscrewed for the potent yellow tablets she took for an asthma attack. I knew what I was doing was inexcusable. I couldn't help myself.

'I haven't finished with you yet, Alex,' she called.

'Don't count on it,' I said, walking away fast. All this ambition to be an obstetrician was making her uppity. I could tell no one, *no one* about my eavesdropping. I wasn't about to tell Julia, friend that she may be, once have been. She could go and have her asthma attacks and do her good works somewhere else.

---

After school, I got on my bike and rode off smartly, to avoid Julia. I needed to swim, to wrap myself round with water, to loosen the tightness in my stomach. I'd been told to stay away from the pool, normally my bolt hole. I could go to the beach, any beach on the waterfront would do.

It took about twenty minutes of riding; or would have had I not gone straight through a red light and straight into the path of a car starting off with the green light. I heard his horn and his brakes scream in protest, heard the rattles as his car bounced back on to its springs. Another foot and I'd have gone underneath. As it was, I swerved myself, fell sideways, bike jangling, leg, elbow, forearm, hands grazing, scraping, sliding to a halt across stones, gravel, asphalt. What little it takes to cause such damage to human skin. I scrambled to my feet as cars piled up behind.

'Beating the gun?' I yelled at the driver, by now out of his car. He was an oldish man, someone's grandad, wearing a brown old man's hat, and I could see he was as shaken as I was. 'Trying to beat the lights? You nearly killed me.'

Pinpricks of blood were appearing in the large areas of raw flesh up my leg. I was so angry I was literally jumping up and down.

He said, 'You went through a red light, girlie.'

'Girlie? What sort of a word is that?'

'Are you all right?'

'No I'm not all right. I've got third-degree grazes and my bike is probably ruined. I suppose I should say thank you for not killing me. Drivers like you get away with murder.'

'You went through a red light,' he repeated, dumbstruck, as I swiped my hands along my tunic, ostentatiously flicked the blood from my legs and elbows (God, it hurt), picked up my bike, and inspected it for damage. All around the intersection faces were watching, people waiting at the lights or behind windscreens. I felt a total fool.

'Girlie, I'm sorry,' he said, grabbing my arm, knowing full well he was in the right. 'But it wasn't my fault ... I've seen you before?'

Yes, in a newspaper or two. This morning's for a start.

'I'm the Tinman from the Wizard of Oz. Knock me down, rub me down with sandpaper, beat me back into shape with a hammer, who cares?' I caught a final glimpse before I rode away. You read about people standing open-mouthed, well he was. I heard him shout something about taking me to a hospital.

I rode about a block before I began to shake so much I had to stop for quite some minutes before I could go on. Besides, I couldn't see the road for tears. Mum's kitchen grater couldn't have done a better job on my legs or elbows, scraped raw like a carrot. How they stung! That little episode was one hundred per cent my fault. Day-dreaming (and going at some speed) through a red light — and nearly another statistic, like ... How much pain had Andrew Trevor Richmond, aged 17, of Kohimarama, killed last night by a hit-and-run driver, how much had he felt? I concentrated on the pain. I was stinging all over; but at least there was nothing broken. I was alive, more's the pity.

There seemed to be no damage to my trusty bike, as we gradually picked up speed. The beach opened up in front of me. I propped my bike against a tree, and flopped on to the grass above the sand. The tide was nearly high, good for swimming, the sea calm, just a summer breeze. On the waterfront road behind, traffic sped past; before me were moored boats, a few people swimming, mothers with picnic baskets and naked babies. Girls sunbathing, dipping in prissy toes. Boys rigging dinghies, boys sailing dinghies.

Why had I come here, this beach? The last time it was blowing a twenty-knot westerly. The Cherub had taken off like a rocket, exhilarating beyond belief. Then for some reason I can't remember I'd got angry with Andy and leapt overboard, intending to swim home, but a mile in a choppy sea, against the wind and an outgoing tide, is not the same as a mile in a pool.

I remember, now. I'd got angry at his message, the real possibility of failure. 'For the rest of my life I'll be the guy who took his girlfriend sailing and d-d-d-drowned her. Can you do that, Alex?' he had yelled, the first time I'd heard him shout in anger. So I'd climbed in, and the sails flogged about while Andy climbed on top of me and we kissed so hard with relief and passion that later I found all sorts of bruises that come from trying to be passionate in a twelve-foot dinghy, and which caused some very ribald comments about love bites at school and at the pool.

The rest of his life. All two weeks of it.

I pulled my togs out of the bag, and looked for a changing-shed. It was down the other end of the beach, so I threw caution and school rules to the winds and changed right there, little caring about modesty, or the areas of bloody raw skin. The water would wash them clean.

Yes, but how they stung as I dived in! Salt water on grated flesh — it may be the best thing for healing, as Mr Jack said afterwards, but you pay a price. My whole body tingled, jangled, resonated like an out-of-tune violin on a very high note.

I'd swum a long way out, fast, furious, long past the nearest moored yachts, and the violin had dropped to a low throbbing beat, when I heard the voice.

'Alex!'

Even here, no peace? A yacht about to run me down as well? Above me a dinghy loomed, its white sail flapping, a gnomish face grinning at me over the side.

Keith Jameson.

'Thought I recognized you. There's only one girl who swims like that.'

How would he know, he's never seen me swim, except maybe that terrible night at Helensville last year; the night four of us went out for a hot swim and he smashed himself and his girlfriend up.

'Great swim in Napier. I read about it in the paper this morning. Did you get my telegram?'

'Yes. Thanks,' I said, treading water. I couldn't imagine why he'd bothered. I hadn't seen him since I climbed out of his car in high dudgeon before the Helensville smash-up, not even at Andy's funeral — had I been in a fit state to recognize anyone?

'Training for Rome, now, are we?'

'No.' I kicked myself into action and began to swim back to the shore. On my breathing strokes, I could see he'd got the yacht sailing and was following me in.

I waded ashore, panting, ignoring him, picked up my towel and patted carefully at my grazes, while he pulled the dinghy up.

'Like to come for a sail?'

'No thanks.'

'Another time? I don't start varsity lectures for another couple of weeks.'

'No.'

'How's your leg?'

'How's yours?'

Both of us had broken legs last year, me one from hockey and him two from his car crash. We eyed each other's legs. His were on the skinny side, and hairy, with prominent knobbly knees, but then he was a wiry type anyway. His eyes travelled up my legs, too slowly for comfort. I now noted the scar down the side of his face (multiple cuts, the paper had said) and more on his neck and shoulders. He hadn't been much of an oil painting to start with.

'You fall off your bike or something?'

'Yes.'

'Looks sore.'

'No.' At least he didn't fuss.

He was fiddling with something on the front wires holding the mast up, not looking at me. 'I crewed for him, sometimes.'

'Who?'

He glanced up, just briefly.

'Oh. I didn't even know you sailed.' I couldn't help asking, 'Is that his boat?'

'No, it's mine. His boat's still sitting outside the house, his parents don't know what to do with it but won't sell it. Too soon, I suppose.'

For all of us. I turned away, picked up my uniform and walked up towards my bike. I didn't feel like dressing on the beach with him staring at me. In his eyes had been the most curious expression, a mirror of my own mixed-up feelings.

He didn't follow. When I came out of the changing-shed the boat was gone. It might have been any one of the five or six dinghies with white sails out there. I envied them their smooth grace through the water, unlike swimming which is basically a lot of splash and hard work. I could be tempted into sailing, given different times and places and people and memories. Home, meanwhile, was a long tiring uphill ride away, and my grazes were wet and seeping blood and hurting like hell.

'Where have you been?' said Mum, preparing dinner as I clomped, very hot and very tired, through the kitchen towards the shower. Unfortunately there was no other way to get there.

'Out.'

'How's school?'

'Horrible. I want to have driving lessons.'

'When the pressure's off.' Peeling spuds, she paused and looked at me. 'Alex, what *have* you been doing? Look at your leg. And elbow!' I'd tried to keep my grated side out of sight, but you can't keep much from Mum.

'Nothing.'

'Nothing, and you've got grazes like that?'

'Like what?' Her jaw went stubborn. 'Riding round on my bike, if you must know. I fell off, that's all.'

Being a nurse she couldn't help it. She dropped her peeler and gave me the once-over. 'Must have been some fall. At least there's not much grit or stones.'

They've all been washed out by the sea, I thought, but I wasn't going to tell her that. My hair had dried to its normal wisps on the way home.

'After you've showered, I'll put some dressings on.'

'I'll be all right.'

'At least the elbow. It's still bleeding.'

'It'll stop. Don't fuss.'

She went back to peeling spuds, grimly. 'Maggie rang. Wants you to call back.'

I have nothing to say to Maggie, I thought as I retreated to the shower. We both know there is a rotten six weeks ahead. We'll have several more well-publicized races, seen by everyone as grudge matches, and we'll both be making extra record attempts as the only way left to convince Messrs Upjohn, Jones and Webster of our worthiness. Tenth of a second by miserable tenth of a second down towards Rome. Or sticking in a rut, growing desperate with failure. And being no saint, I'm certainly not going to tell her what I overheard, that if she managed to break my time 'substantially' she'd be back level pegging with me.

When I finally and reluctantly rang later, Maggie shamed me into an admission of shared disappointment. The selectors, she said, hadn't been much help, had they? From her weaker position, she could still say *I* deserved a nomination. 'We both do,' I said, admiring her generosity. Her mother, apparently, was furious, though I'd have thought she might also be relieved that the door was still open. I wondered if she'd started to pull strings, complain, and carry on. 'How's school?' I said. 'I didn't go today.' Interesting, couldn't she face it, the embarrassment of people saying, great race, Maggie, sorry you lost? She didn't elaborate; I wondered just what was going on in the Benton household.

Sorry, Maggie. You really are a much nicer person than me, and it will be great if we both go to Rome together. But this, meanwhile, is a parting of the ways.

In one of the city's older suburbs, on the lower slopes of a green terraced volcano rising up from the harbour, a vigil had been kept.

The house was typical of the area: two storeyed, with gleaming white weatherboards, set back from the street in a spacious garden of lawn, rose-beds, and old Empire trees planted a hundred years earlier by the gardener wives of settlers. Australian eucalypts, Indian deodars and English oaks stood alongside native tree-fern, cabbage-tree, puriri, kowhai, rimu, and pohutukawa.

It was perhaps also typical that the owner, the provider for this family, should be away overseas, in Singapore or maybe London, on one of his frequent business trips. Maggie was used to her father's absences, to his rarely being around to share her triumphs or her disappointments, and she would not have turned to him for comfort this night, either. At midnight, with a nagging headache from the long silent drive back from Napier, and unable to sleep, she had swallowed the two pills her mother gave her — aspirin, she was told — and been grateful to drift off at last into a restless sleep.

Joyce Benton spent the rest of the night among the carved rosewood furniture and fine Oriental vases of her living room, in preference to the large and lonely bed upstairs. She read, knitted, put on a long-playing record of Mantovani and sipped several gins. She dozed a little, confident that two of her own regular sleeping pills would keep Maggie's head on the pillow until mid-morning.

Mostly she just sat and thought, filling up the ashtray on the coffee table. She went endlessly over the selectors' options. Send just Alex, or send both, or send neither. She no longer had any illusions that Maggie could be the sole nominee. Training in Australia, expensive coaching; Maggie's talent, body and temperament nurtured as carefully as any thoroughbred — and still that uncouth, wretched girl had come out on top, sabotaging her Olympic plans. She had already booked her own air ticket and confidently written to Italian friends from Singapore days: 'You will of course remember our Margaret, once champion at the club. To our great joy and delight, after many years of hard work, we fully expect her to be selected to swim for New Zealand in the two freestyle events at Rome in August.' With any luck, an offer of accommodation would come by return.

If both girls are both nominated, she reasoned, both must be selected finally, or neither. The selectors would be unlikely to name one female swimmer, requiring two officials, both manager and chaperon, unless the case for sending that swimmer were irrefutable. Until Saturday night Maggie had enough edge over Alex to have been that one. Growing chill in her housecoat of ming embroidered silk, she got up to make a cup of tea. The first light of dawn meant the paper must be here soon.

When she finally heard the squeak of the boy's bicycle, she delayed walking down the drive to the gate, and delayed opening the paper she pulled from the letter-box. She stopped to smell some roses, and bent to pull out a few tiny weeds in the brick driveway. Inside the house, she put the paper on the sofa, poured another cup of tea, lit another cigarette and ran her eye over the front page. Yet more church leaders complaining about the exclusion of Maoris in the All Black tour to South Africa; yet more about Harold Macmillan and his 'winds of change' speech to the South African Parliament. Then she turned abruptly to the sports pages and quickly found what she wanted.

Cowards, she thought angrily, cowards hiding behind a smokescreen of pompous generalities, prolonging the agony. It was also humiliating; these girls are not yet quite good enough, it told the world. But between the lines there was hope, a message that Alex's win on Saturday had not clinched the matter, and that Maggie was still in with a chance.

Joyce Benton sat on for another half an hour, chain-smoking, thinking, until Maggie's ten-year-old sister Isabel come wandering down the stairs wanting breakfast.

'Don't wake your sister,' she said. Why were you crying last night, said the child; I went to the toilet and you were down here crying. You were dreaming, said her mother sharply. Did Maggie, asked Isabel, get nominated? No one did, and won't be for another six weeks, said her mother. That's not fair, said Isabel. Six weeks *more*, creeping around, don't upset your sister, thought Isabel.

'Don't wake your sister,' said her mother. 'Your uniform is in the laundry.' Maggie could sleep herself out this morning. She would ring the school to explain.

Meanwhile, the delay could be useful, thought Joyce Benton as she carefully poached eggs and cut toast into even slender fingers. She would never get used to having to prepare her own breakfast, rather than having it brought to her on a tray with fine Chinese linen by the amah. The phone went several times, quite possibly Alex, she thought sourly, lifting and replacing the receiver. There were several carnivals planned, there must be time trials, record attempts, school pressures on Maggie made minimal; she must speak to the headmistress. As for Alex, there were a number of interesting avenues to be explored.

---

So, again the treadmill. School, training at five in the morning and again after school, sleeping badly, losing yet more weight; training and more training and my grazes, immersed twice a day in water, growing infected, scabby, itchy, slowly eventually healing; dreading upcoming races and record attempts in the full glare of publicity.

I am living two lives, two lies: the routine daily world of pain, dragging myself from pool to school to home, avoiding contact, snapping at almost everybody. Except Mr Jack. He doesn't say much either, but he's *there*, my anchor on the side of the pool, nodding quietly when I do a good time trial and ignoring the bad ones. I cry for no apparent reason. It's high summer, day after day of beautiful weather, but I'm either inside a classroom or ploughing through water. I get no joy from the sun.

Then there's the other, public life, the fantasy world of being 'a celebrity'. I refuse most of the requests I get, and know that most of the people think me ungrateful and arrogant for doing so. For example, please help our fund-raising campaign for a new swimming pool or school hall. Ten invitations to speak to women's groups and school assemblies, seven to give out the silver cups and certificates at swimming clubs' end-of-season prize-givings.

I write a lot of polite refusal notes.

Mr Jack will not allow me to avoid the Press entirely. I am, he says, a public figure: my fare to Rome will be paid by public money and for that I have certain obligations. I have two radio interviews and a colour picture taken for the *Women's Weekly*, to go with a long article about all the female Olympic hopefuls, athletes (who have already been nominated) and swimmers (who have not). 'Please,' the editor writes, 'could you also write something for our Teenage Pages — how you manage to be a champion sportswoman and still keep your femininity?' Sorry, no I couldn't, because I'm not an expert on femininity, and do not want to be reminded about my alleged lack of same.

There were nuttier ones, to open a garden fête and judge a baby competition, a teenage beauty queen competition, and a talent quest for the best Shirley Temple or Elvis Presley imitations — all of which filled me with horror. 'On the Good Ship Lollipop' would be *the* most nauseating song ever written, without a doubt; and I can't *bear* Elvis.

'Here's one I think you should accept,' said Mum, as I came in from training. 'A Mr Brookefield from Rotary rang, wants both you and Maggie to speak at a special luncheon next month.'

'Because her father is a member, I suppose.'

'That's not the point.'

'Tell them no.'

'I think you should.'

'Why?'

'Rotary is . . . influential. Very choosy about its members and its speakers.'

'We should feel flattered, you mean.'

'No I don't mean. For the sake of your sport, you should go. It's to honour the achievement of youth, he said.'

'And I suppose Mrs Benton will be there.'

'Very likely. We've been invited too.'

Could I stand it, after seeing her face the night I beat Maggie? I'd heard on the grapevine that there'd been some hard words hissed at Maggie's coach as my name came over as winner, and more as the crowd left the stands. The Aussie coach brought over at great expense had made the mistake of admiring my fighting spirit, and been virtually told to go back to where he came from.

Later that night she had walked past me twice, nose in the air, before dragging Maggie away from the party very early. At training since then I'd seen her only, by mutual agreement, across the other side of the pool.

'When is it, this Rotary thing?'

'March 27, in town. Lunch, then a panel discussion.'

By then the die would probably be cast. 'All right,' I said ungraciously. Had I known that Mr Upjohn would be there too, I would not have allowed myself to be persuaded quite so easily. Or at all. He had just been announced as the Manager for the swimming team to Rome, along with a Mrs Churchill from Christchurch, who I knew slightly, as chaperon. It struck me as very odd (and Mr Jack smiled when I said so) that they chose the officials before the competitors. I thought we were the ones who actually did the competing, that the Games were held for us. Did that mean they really did intend to send *someone*?

'Your hair needs a cut,' said Mum. 'If you're going to wear it that short . . .'

'Costs too much,' I said, flouncing out. 'You're always going on about money.' I looked at myself in my dressing-table mirror. She was right, it was all ends. I dropped on to my bed. Under the pillow was a small silver frame, courtesy of Gran, with the picture of me and Andy taken by Dad at Muriwai last year, just as we came back from a passionate lunch in the black sand dunes.

'Will you wait for me . . .?' I looked at it for a while, with a great empty hole where my heart should be.

So my hair needed a cut. Why spend good money when all they did was snip off bits around the ends. I could do that. So I sneaked a pair of Gran's dressmaking scissors from her room while she was helping chase Debbie into bed, and did the deed myself. I tried to even out the sides, and get the fringe straight; it turned out shorter and scraggier than I intended, sort of Roman. It'll grow, who cared.

Despite all those people out there who want me to judge this, open that or present the other, reassuring me that of course I'm going (with Mr Upjohn and Mrs Churchill) to Rome to swim against Dawn Fraser and see the Colosseum, I feel, I *know* that I am the most gigantic empty sham.

It was pouring summer rain on the asphalt of the netball courts outside, and the worms were out. Around me the Sixth Form English class groaned. Desk lids flew open noisily, with mutterings of 'Bor-ring . . . that old creep . . . George Bernard who? . . . here we go again, the Mackerel on her drama kick . . . wake me when the bell goes.'

'One of the greatest plays of the twentieth century,' Miss Macrae announced briskly. 'Settle down, girls. Alex, where's your book?'

I'd been gazing at her while all the scuffling was going on. Saint Joan — hadn't she once been Joan in London? And for some reason after that she'd stopped acting and become a teacher in the colonies? Today she was not in any mood for messing around. My fearsome haircut had occasioned only a long cool appraisal. 'Alex, are you with us? We haven't got all day. Have you looked at this yet?'

Shaking my head, I got out my Penguin *Saint Joan*. I had read it, the whole thing, including sixty-nine pages of Preface. It was funny and tragic and the bits in the Preface about women through history who wanted to wear men's clothes simply because they wanted to lead a man's life, either in disguise or by defying public opinion, was the first bit of good sense on the subject I'd ever read. And written in 1924!

'We'll go straight to the script, and come back to the Preface later,' Miss Macrae announced. 'Now come on girls, backs straight, you are about to meet one of the most fascinating minds in English literature.'

'Weren't you Joan once?' said a voice.

'Yes, I played Joan.'

'How did they burn you up on the stage, like when they burned Ingrid Bergman?'

'They didn't. Shaw's fire is more effectively described through the eyes of a young French monk and the English chaplain, her most implacable enemy. Put that letter away please Monica — or would you like to share it with the class?' The class grinned hopefully.

'In the film it was horrible. You could see . . .'

'We are studying Shaw, not Hollywood. Now who's going to read what?'

I knew what I wanted. But the parts came and went and I ended up Dunois. 'He's twenty-six,' said Miss Macrae, 'the French commander. Capable, good-natured, a staunch supporter of Joan. Alex, you can read that.'

And Joan went to Kathie who certainly had Shaw's 'uncommon face' but not much else. I loathed these class readings. Most people hadn't got a clue and it was wooden and tediously slow and no wonder people got put off Shakespeare and Shaw and Wilde and the other people we had to study. It struck me that Miss Macrae must have similar urges to stop people and say for heaven's sake put some life into it, read it as though you mean it. These are human beings talking. Kathie was pathetic, milk and water.

I sat back and listened with scorn, until at one particularly feeble bit which wouldn't have inspired an army of mice let alone French soldiers, I caught a very strange look from the teacher's desk, a flicker of a knowing smile that said, 'I agree. Painful. You'd do it better.' Yes, I thought angrily, and you couldn't even give me the pleasure of just reading the part, just once. Dunois didn't even appear until the third scene, which would not be in today's English period. Maybe in about three weeks at this rate. I put my chin on my cupped hands and ostentatiously dozed off, and had to be woken when the bell went. Miss Macrae equally ostentatiously turned a blind eye. I had another race with Maggie that night and needed the sleep.

When Maggie Benton beat Alex Archer for the third time in special invitation races up in Auckland, lowering the women's sprint record by three-tenths of a second and making sports headlines even in his local Napier paper, Grant Davies knew he could remain silent no longer.

'Maggie comes back fighting,' said the caption to a large picture in the Auckland paper which showed Alex congratulating an elated Maggie. Was he imagining despair in those wondrous grey eyes, Grant mused, sitting at the long reporters' desk in the newsroom, ploughing through the morning papers from all round the country. During that remarkable interview after her win at the nationals, he'd seen her dutiful, a little bored, and then, as they listened to the voices, seen her grow wide-eyed and flushed with determination to control her shame and anger. There was something distant and formidable about her, a larger-than-life quality which put out of reach any expectations a cub reporter like himself might have about getting to know her better, even had they lived in the same town. The accompanying report speculated yet again about the equal Olympic chances of each. Since the writer was no ordinary journo, but Norman Thompson, the country's best-known and most influential sports reporter, Grant took some comfort. Yet it was not enough to counter his growing sense of guilt and conviction that he had to tell someone what was going on.

Cub reporters don't normally get sent on assignments to Auckland, thought Grant, and so it turned out. The chief reporter was not impressed with a proposal that his admittedly brightest but also youngest and newest sports reporter should be sent to Auckland to cover an international tennis tournament. So it happened that Grant Davies, who'd never been outside Napier or slept in any bed other than his own, left the next morning ostensibly to go to work and from a telephone booth at the deserted Napier bus terminal rang in sick to the early duty newsroom copy typist. 'A bad dose of 'flu,' he said, surprised by his convincing croak, 'high fever, don't expect I'll be in for two or three days. Tell the Chief someone'll have to do my council meeting tomorrow night.' He knew, with his reputation for punctuality and completing assignments on time and staying away from the pub, a bit of a mummy's boy, he'd be believed without question. To his mother, he made a call saying he was going away unexpectedly to Auckland for a few days, his first big assignment, something to do with the All Black tour to South Africa. She was naturally very proud.

'I must be crazy,' he thought as the near-empty bus climbed over the unsealed, rutted and tortuous road to Taupo. What the hell am I going to tell Norm Thompson, who probably won't even remember that I sat behind him in the Press box at the national championships? That Alex Archer's chances of getting to Rome are nil, the chief selector hates her guts. She knows it, and I've heard it with my own ears. What can he, we, do about it anyway?

By Taupo, Grant had convinced himself that nothing much could be done and that he was on a wild goose chase. It would take all day to get to Auckland, and another whole day to get back. Napier was such a small damn place, his boss was bound to find out, or his mother. Yet he knew why he hadn't done the more sensible thing and used the telephone. He wanted to see what a city newsroom looked like, he wanted to see where the legendary Norm Thompson worked, and he knew from Norm's piece in the *Herald* that Alex and Maggie were both having their final record attempts during the coming week. And he couldn't live with himself if Alex with the steely grey wounded eyes missed out on the Olympic team and he'd not told someone what he knew.

---

Time is running out. At dawn training, and again as we finish at dusk, there is a feeling of autumn in the air. Between Maggie and me, training where possible at different times, it's frosty; between Mrs Benton (hanging round the pool like a bad smell) and me, it's positively polar.

We race together five times. Apart from old Norm Thompson in the *Herald* who keeps harping on that the selectors must send us both, the press writes a lot of nonsense about revenge, and organizers advertise the meetings as Olympics hopefuls fighting it out to the death. We win two each. Somehow I've stopped caring, until the last race which Maggie wins, taking a whole *substantial* point four off my record.

'I think we'd better have an official record attempt, Alex,' says Mr Jack, after the race. 'The pool's closing on Sunday. I'll ask for Thursday.'

On Thursday there's a small crowd of officials and swimmers gathered to watch. Not Maggie, though I see her mother sitting on the stands by herself. Come to gloat, stick pins in my wax effigy, I dare say. The water looks unfriendly too, and there's a chill wind blowing the length of the pool. I have a sore throat, I'm half a stone lighter, it doesn't feel right at all, and I miss her record by point one.

'So you missed. It's still a personal best, faster than Napier. And this is a slower pool than Napier, don't forget,' says Mr Jack as I climb hurting from the pool. 'It was a great swim Alex, and I know you can do a sixty-three. We'll ask for another crack at the weekend.'

He doesn't tell me that Messrs Upjohn, Jones and Webster would be there, along with a much bigger crowd (because word has got about) come to see both me *and* Maggie have our final desperate fling in the long-course pool.

We warm up on opposite sides of the pool, and join our coaches on opposite sides. Neither of us suggests we make a race of it. My whole family sits in a gloomy row, probably sick to death of me and who could blame them. I walk about, numb with nerves. I see Norm Thompson with a photographer and some young guy who looks vaguely familiar. Despite his neat clothes, there is something about him that says Press, and something about the way he stares that makes me uneasy. Where have I met him before?

'Who's going first?' asks the chief timekeeper. Neither of us can look up. I'm about to say, I'd rather go second when he says, 'Toss for it, then?' Too late. The seconds tick by while he finds a coin, flicks it, drops it, flicks again. Couldn't he have thought of something more appropriate, less flippant? Despite my dry togs and a jumper under my track suit, and socks, I'm shivering with cold. The sun has gone behind the stands; the water is a hostile flat icy blue.

'Maggie, call?'

'Tails,' she says.

He lifts his palm and we all peer at the Maori warrior squatting on a silver shilling, spear at the ready. 'Tails it is. Your choice, Maggie.'

'I'll swim second,' she says, and they all turn to look at me. Damn your eyes, Maggie. You would. I would have too, given the choice. I'm not quite ready to throw my last card. I'm feeling sick and my shoulders are tight, and annoyed that I cannot remember where I've met that face before. I go into the dressing room for a pee, and find myself retching over the toilet bowl.

When I come out, trembling, there stands Mrs Benton, combing her already immaculate perm. She looks at me in the mirror. I had not heard her high heels on the tiled floor. She is not there by accident.

'Are you all right, Alex?' she says, with more curiosity than concern. She almost certainly heard the unpleasant noises coming from the toilet.

I turn my back to wash my hands and sluice my sweating brow with water. Even if I was dying, you are the last person . . .

I am not, not, *not* going to talk to you.

*Napier!* I remember now. The earnest lad with his carefully prepared questions, writing hesitant shorthand, his Adam's apple moving up and down behind a staid tie, the long silent corridor echoing with selectors' voices. Why am I bothering? As I lean over the basin, I am shaking uncontrollably all over.

'Are you well enough to swim, Alex? You look quite overwrought. If you were my daughter, I'd be putting my foot down.'

Since she has invaded my privacy, I'll make it worthwhile, give her something to remember. I retch disgustingly into the basin and spit out a mouthful of yellowish saliva as noisily and revoltingly as I know how. Not a pretty sight, I'm sure.

She waits. Then she says, quite blandly, matter-of-fact and all the more menacing for it, 'Maggie will swim well under sixty-four today, I believe. She did a sixty-three point nine at training last night. You may not have heard.'

Oh, I heard all right. You don't keep times like that secret. But I will *not* give her the satisfaction of a response. I straighten up, give her a brief, dismissive glance, wipe my wet face with my towel, have a final hoick and spit in the basin and walk out. Her face was as blank as her voice. Don't you know *yet*, Mrs Benton, I am a dangerous animal when aroused.

'Take your time, Alex,' murmurs Mr Jack as I stride over to the starting blocks and throw off my track suit. I watch myself from a great height checking my cap, swinging arms, shaking legs, filling my lungs with air as I walk around behind the block, back and forth, like a big caged cat.

The face beside Norm Thompson clicks into focus; he gives a sober sort of half grin and a small thumbs up gesture. Afterwards, I have to admit it was a good reminder of what's at stake and what I have to overcome. I storm up to the block and glare at the starter. I can't wait to get in the water. I have become a shark.

I know from the shouts and the timekeepers' faces that it's good. As they compare stop-watches, Mr Jack comes hurtling over and as he kneels down to show me his watch, his face is a joy.

'I make it sixty-three point eight,' says Mr Jack, hoarsely. When the official time is announced, he's spot on. I can't help looking over at Mr Upjohn, who is sitting in the front row of the stand with his chin in his hands, nodding thoughtfully as Albie Jones talks and searches through his files to make a point. He sees my look: Put that in your pipe. My complete family, all six of them, leave their seats and surround me.

Though it was her choice to go second, it's awful for Maggie, the cheers and general jubilation. Now the pressure is all hers. Her mother and coach are giving her final instructions, stupidly. She'd have been better walking about quietly, psyching herself up, concentrating on the two laps to come. I watch her curiously as she prepares, gives her mother her jumper, track suit bottoms, track suit top, socks. As she comes over to the block I think she's holding back tears. She looks very small in her black racers, and very lonely. She's slow off the blocks; but through the smooth water looks so fast and graceful that I'm struck with a sense of wonder that I must look every bit as powerful. I watch Mrs Benton at the turn — the lap time is clearly too slow. She goes stone-faced as people around us start shouting encouragement. Over the last ten yards I see the stop-watch held high, counting off the seconds — sixty-one, sixty-two, sixty-three . . . sixty-four? Sixty-three point . . . what? I can't watch. That a trip to the other side of the world should hang on a tenth of a second.

'Sixty-four point one,' says Mr Jack, unable to keep the glee out of his voice. Equalling her official personal best, but not mine.

'Of course I am relieved, and pleased. But I'm not so mean that I don't feel sorry for Maggie, who comes over to give me a hug with a grim rueful smile, mercifully unaware of her own mother's part in all this. Her mother, I note, (to whom I suppose I should be grateful) is ear-bashing the coach again. I see Norm Thompson talking to Mr Jack. The lad from Napier comes over, and shakes my hand.

'Grant Davies, from Napier,' he says, looking me dead straight in the eye. 'A great swim, better even than Napier.'

'What are you doing up in Auckland?'

'Interviews,' he says. 'Meeting people.'

'Interviewed Maggie?' I say. 'Or Mrs Benton? She's always got a lot to say.'

'I'm here for the tennis. But it's good to see you book your place for Rome.'

'Oh, yes? We'll see.' He'd kept his promise of silence, as far as I knew. I suddenly feel very tired of all these games and battles, and have to sit down. I've played my last card, Maggie. If I were you I'd have one further throw. She does try again, the next day, on the eve of pool closing. And equals my time. Mr Jack, who rings to tell me this, says that my advantage has narrowed down to the sprint title I won in Napier, against Maggie's greater reliability. You're a tough nut, Maggie old girl, a real battler.

Is this an official time, I ask, with proper timekeepers and all? Or just her mother and her drippy coach.

Official, he says. Cyril Upjohn was there. No doubt, I say, cheering her on. Are you suggesting out and out favouritism, Alex? I'm tempted to say yes, let me tell you about Napier, but what's the bloody point? I laugh into the phone before I hang up and start howling.

Bill Jack put the telephone down slowly in his small, sparsely furnished office at the pool, which featured only a large framed aerial photograph, rather garishly hand-coloured, taken during events at the 1950 Empire Games ten years earlier.

Today he was closing down the pool for the winter; it was an unsatisfactory and depressing note to end a season on. Swimming was supposed to be a fun thing, a useful and health-giving skill for children, but for his star pupil, and to only a slightly lesser degree, for Maggie, it had developed into an ongoing struggle that would have finished many an older competitor.

He was deeply disturbed by the bitterness in Alex's voice. 'So that's it,' she said. 'Perhaps the selectors will toss for it. Heads Maggie goes, tails I stay behind. Perhaps they just don't want me in Rome.'

He had at that point wavered, torn by respect for her secret, and anger at what he had two days earlier heard off the record from Norm Thompson turning up late in the afternoon, supposedly to watch training. A young reporter, Grant someone from the paper in Hawkes Bay, had turned up at the sports desk out of the blue, said Norm. Straight off the bus from Napier. He was a serious, unlikely young man, not your normal sports journo. He said he'd been with Alex the night of the nationals, an hour after her victory, and had listened to some dark and uncomplimentary statements on the part of the selectors. This would explain the delay in nominations and could be interpreted as a devious manoeuvre to favour Maggie, and put Alex out of the running. This lad, said Norm, had been sitting on this quite unusable story for several weeks, while Maggie closed the gap on her no doubt demoralized rival. Even now, I'm damned if I know what can be done, Norm had said, other than to pass it on as useful background to you, to use as you see fit.

She's not breathed a word of this to me, said Bill Jack hopelessly, watching Alex and Maggie and the few swimmers still left in the pool so late in the day, but it explained a lot. To aspiring swimmers, the selectors were the next thing to God almighty, their deliberations secret, and their decisions final.

Norm, snorting cynically, said well, I could tackle Cyril Upjohn but he's a slippery customer, would simply deny the lot, say it was the overheated imagination of a foolish young girl or an unprincipled reporter fabricating a good story. Young Grant said that Alex begged him not to tell anyone. Even if he'd tackled Cyril, and blown the story himself, it would only have backfired on Alex. She was quite right, a clever girl. Sorry, Bill old man, I hope your knowing helps get the kid to Rome. God knows she deserves it. My granddaughter goes ga-ga at even the mention of her name. I'm a bit of a fan myself.

In the end, after much thought, Bill Jack had decided not to tell Alex that word of her secret had got back, even though it had been passed on by people who believed in fair play and wanted to see her win her place for Rome. For whatever reason, she decided not to share her dark burden; not with him, nor apparently, with her parents. As if she didn't have enough on her young shoulders already. After Norm Thompson had left the pool, Bill Jack went out on to the concourse and felt a chill wind and tears prick his eyes as he watched over two lonely and troubled girls still ploughing up and down in the gathering autumn dusk.

---

'I'm bloody sick of this.'

'Jamie, mind your language.'

'Why's it not in the paper this morning?'

'Don't point your knife at me, little boy.'

'Why's it not?'

He's a persistent little creep.

'Because the selectors haven't decided, that's why.'

'Why not? They said six weeks, it's six weeks today and I'm sick of it.'

'*You're* sick of it!'

'Finished breakfast, Jamie?' calls Gran from the sink. 'I'd like some help with the chooks.'

Jamie makes another accusing stab with his breadknife at me.

'She was up at five, out at the gate, waiting for the paper.'

'I'm always up at five.'

'I saw you.'

'So?'

'Jamie, for heaven's sake, leave her alone,' says Dad from behind his newspaper. 'Go and help Gran.'

'You just want to get rid of me.'

'Too bloody right,' I shout. 'Piss off.'

Silence. Gran takes Jamie by the hand and leads him out. Mum and Dad are gritting their teeth. Debbie and Robbie are head down into their cornflakes. Since I can't eat a thing, I see no point in prolonging this.

'Alex . . .' Mum begins, overture to a familiar dirge. I could write the script: we know it's hard, it's hard on us too, please eat some breakfast, please stop cutting your hair in that awful way, please tidy up your room, please stop picking at the quicks of your nails, please stop swearing at your brother, please put your jeans out for a wash, please wear something normal for a change, like a dress, please try to meet your teachers half-way, please try to forget Andy, please . . .

'Forget it.'

The nominations were not in this morning's paper. They are not in tonight's *Star*. Oh, they know how to twist the knife, these people. They are not in Tuesday's papers, nor Wednesday's. I am not training, what's the point now, until I know one way or t'other. I can't sleep, can't eat. I sit in class in a daze, and after school dawdle home and lock myself in my bedroom. Sometimes I play the piano, every piece I've ever learnt and some of the songs from the shows I've been in. I'm missing my music, I realize. Once or twice I nearly ring Julia, but she's been pretty stand-offish. Maggie? What could we say to each other? More platitudes. Or to her bloody mother if she answered the phone? I sometimes get a clear picture of three men sitting round smoking pipes, Mr Upjohn using all his greasy charm to convince the others I should not be nominated. I don't want her in Rome. But I hold the title and share the record, how much is enough?

Mr Jack rings once or twice, he means well, but what can he say? Keith rings, because he actually noticed that Norm Thompson's last bit in Monday's *Herald* said that the nominations were expected this week, and noticed that it was dragging on. Strange.

Even stranger, a toll call from Napier along much the same lines, from baby-faced Grant Davies. 'Norm Thompson has promised me he'll ring you when anything comes through from the Press Association, so you'll get it early.' Why, I wonder, is old Norm promising favours to a cub reporter from Napier, young enough to be his grandson? I nearly ask him if he blabbed, but again, now, what is the point? 'You'll make it,' says Grant. 'Good luck.'

Thursday afternoon and I am nearly climbing the wall. After school the thought of my own company behind a locked bedroom door is too much, and I need a long sweat-making burn out. My bike finds its own way towards a certain house, a quiet side street. The garage is open. His parents must be out, in the Volkswagen where we once ... Through the open door at the back of the garage I can see into the garden, and his yacht, forlorn on a trailer. I don't know how long I sit there, until I hear a car coming up the hill: the throaty sound of the Volkswagen home for tea. I swing my bike around and grunt on up the hill, hoping they had not recognized me. If I ever needed you it was now, Andy Richmond. Why, why ... damn you, and Maggie and her sixty-three point eight and her miserable conniving mother and those pompous old selectors and the stupid Olympic Games, damn, damn, damn everything ...

That night the phone goes. Late. The house is asleep and I'm reading Tolstoy, *Anna Karenina*, and crying into the pages, because I know how it ends.

I know immediately who it is. I can't get out of bed.

Mum answers promptly, years (she says) of responding to cries of children, and patients when she was a nurse. She knocks on my door. 'Alex? For you.'

I can't move. 'Alex!'

'Coming.' It's all slow motion again.

'Do you want me to leave you alone?'

'Yes.' Please. I don't want anyone listening, watching. 'I'm coming.' She goes back to the phone and tells Norm Thompson she's coming, please hang on.

So I walk along down the dark hallway, only the dim night-light on above me. Mum has closed the door, but a strip of light tells me she's waiting. Pictures I haven't noticed in years appear sharp and important; the runner carpet is worn. Ahead lies the waiting phone on a small table. It takes me about a year to pick it up.

'Alex? Norm Thompson from the *Herald*.'

'Oh, hi.'

'It's just come through on the wire. You're in. Maggie too.'

Oh. I'm nailed to the floor.

'Congratulations. Well deserved. Are you there, Alex?'

'Oh, yes. Thanks.' I can barely get the words out. 'Ah, listen, would you ring Maggie for me? Please.'

'If you want. Got a number?'

'Ah, I can't remember. It's, um, Benton, Seascape Road, Remuera.'

'You wouldn't rather . . .'

'No. Just . . . thanks for ringing,' and I put the phone down very quickly before he can start to ask me for quotes and how I feel because I'm about to weep buckets, and it's Mum's bed that I weep them over, a ten stone, five foot ten and a quarter inch baby that creeps into her bed and cries herself to sleep.

The phone starts ringing before breakfast. Mr Jack is first, even before the paper arrives which means Norm rang him too; obviously so relieved and pleased his smile almost bends the telephone wires. He even hints that he might be able to save enough money to come to Rome. After that, the phone goes non-stop: women officials I've known for years, swimmers, neighbours, relations out of the woodwork on toll calls from Christchurch and Timaru and Napier and Nelson.

I can't get through to Maggie. She's engaged, or it rings once and then clicks off, a fault somewhere, infuriating. I'd always known, way deep down, I was going to Rome, and Maggie too. I want to share it with her.

It's in the paper, in black and white (I feared it might all have been a bad dream) along with some nice comment from Norm Thompson: the selectors are to be commended for doing the decent thing, etcetera. And yet — not much improved from days gone past. While I smile sweetly down the telephone, I hear the kids bitching at each other, and Mum short-tempered. The newspaper is full of 67 DEAD IN SHARPEVILLE after South African police fired on a whole lot of Africans, and MORE CALLS for our All Blacks not to go and play rugby in such a place.

I want to wag school, to escape Miss Gillies' gushing at assembly and the pack of Third Formers that follows me everywhere. I'm feeling guilty about Julia, and bad about being rude to Miss Macrae several times this week. Mr Richmond rings up to offer his congratulations and I find I don't have much to say to him either. 'Andy always knew you'd swim in Rome,' he says, reducing me to a speechless jelly. I seem to have run out of the right responses, the right words to say. Only Gran seems to have any idea of how confused I'm feeling, as I kiss goodbye and tears spring to my eyes. 'To thine own self be true,' she murmurs in my ear.

The weather has turned nasty — a howling nor'easter which is ripping all the leaves off the oaks and cherry trees unseasonably early, while Gran bemoans the state of the garden and Dad can't mow the lawn because it's too wet for our ancient motor mower. We have lit our first fire of the year. It's winter, but I didn't have a summer. Tomorrow morning there'll be the usual picture in the paper of a yacht torn from its harbour moorings and battered to pieces on the waterfront rocks.

I'm feeling a touch battered, a touch adrift myself.

Tomorrow morning I have to start training again.

# Part Two

'TELL me,' said Joyce Benton lightly, 'about Alex.'

The question was primarily aimed at one of her guests, but there was a general reaction of surprise from the five women gathered for morning coffee in the spacious drawing room. Late summer roses, picked that morning during a short break in the rain, stood a little limply in silver bowls; the pale blue carpet and drapes perfectly set off the heavy black Oriental furniture.

'Surely,' said one, 'you know her well enough already, after all these years? This is a beautiful piece, Joyce,' she added, running her fingers over the ornate carvings of the huge coffee table. 'Singapore?'

'From Shanghai, antique,' said Joyce Benton. 'Only in the context of swimming, and now it's likely they'll be travelling together ...'

'You must be so proud of Maggie,' cried another.

'Naturally, but she's worked for it, sacrificed a great deal. So has Alex, such a talented girl, I gather.'

She let the statement linger, not looking directly at her principal target. As she hoped, another took the cue.

'Isn't she a good friend of your daughter, Pauline?'

Julia's mother, leaning forward to pick up the Wedgwood cup, played for time. 'Well, she has been. They seem to have drifted apart of late. Alex has become so obsessed — no, perhaps that's not fair — single-*minded* about her swimming, she doesn't seem to have much time for her old friends.'

Mrs Benton nodded understandingly, and let the conversation flow on.

'What a wonderful experience for them both. Rome in high summer! My husband was there in '44 with the Allies, one of the first to enter the city. He's always wanted to go back, such a historical place, full of arches and tombs and churches, said he'd take me when ...'

'I suppose there's a chaperon,' said another, tackling a hefty slice of chocolate log with her cake fork. 'I shouldn't be eating this, Joyce.'

'Certainly there is. A Mrs Churchill, from Christchurch. I haven't met her, but I'm told she's a very nice woman. Harold and I intend to be there too.'

'I know a Churchill, a lawyer in Christchurch.' Jane Sutherland dug deep into the moist confection on her plate. She was, if not the slimmest, certainly the smartest woman in the room, with aspirations as an organizer of fashion parades and some small successes with charity parades behind her. 'Perhaps his wife?'

'Quite possibly,' said Joyce Benton, knowing full well that the Churchill woman in question was a widow with two teenage sons, and earned her own living as a primary school teacher.

'It's a big responsibility, taking two very attractive girls to Rome. Christopher met Alex at a dance, oh, last May holidays. He was very taken with her. I gather she's very striking?'

Joyce Benton smiled warmly at Mrs Allardyce, whose husband was a member of the City Council and thus worth knowing. 'Very. Rather broad-shouldered, but so was Esther Williams, wasn't she? How does she manage at school, Pauline?'

'She did very well in School Certificate, Julia said, with practically no work. Over-committed, into everything. And last year she was learning ballet, until she broke her leg. Piano too, and getting involved in school shows . . .'

'Really, I didn't know that,' said Joyce Benton. 'In the chorus?'

'Alex in the chorus?' Pauline laughed. 'My dear, she's larger-than-life. We were there the final night of *The Wizard of Oz*. She nearly brought the house down.' On the whole, Pauline McGregor was not sorry Alex had stopped coming to their house; she found the child disconcertingly direct, even aggressive, a questionable influence on Julia, especially on Julia's unfortunate ambition to do medicine, which for some unfathomable reason her father was encouraging; but there was nevertheless something about the girl, something you warmed to.

'Really. So versatile, I hadn't realized. And what does she want to do with all this talent?'

'Law, I believe.'

'Law? That's most unusual. Few women do law.'

'That's probably why,' said Pauline rather pointedly. 'Though there's no doubt she's got the brain for it. She's a prefect too, a popular one. Almost certainly head girl if she stays for the Upper Sixth.'

'Well,' murmured Joyce Benton. 'I look forward to getting to know her better, now. She'll be a stimulating companion for Maggie in Rome.'

Mrs Allardyce said, 'I suppose they're both training very hard again?'

'They started yesterday, in that dreadful indoor pool in town. Twice a day.'

Murmurs of sympathy went around the room. Imagine. Such dedication, you too Joyce, up at five every morning.

'It's very tough. The final selection is about seven weeks away. I have no doubt both will get in the team.'

'How wonderful.'

'How will Maggie cope with School Certificate this year, if she goes to Rome?'

'We're not quite sure she'll even sit at this stage.' She took the chocolate log and orange sponge around a second time, noting how easy it was to persuade her plumper guests into a second — and third — piece, despite their protests and well-informed but ultimately ludicrous talk of diets. The conversation drifted off to other teenage sons and daughters, the dances that were being held in the May holidays, by whom and with whom and where. Television transmission was starting in June, and opinion was divided as to whether to acquire a set sooner, or later; expensive, of course, but having seen it overseas, wonderful for news items, and documentaries too. Of course, the Olympics would be televised. Joyce Benton hadn't given it much thought, since she and Harold were going to be there anyway.

And although it pained her to be reminded of that dreadful night of defeat in Napier, Joyce Benton had left lying casually on the coffee table a large print of the newspaper picture of Maggie and Alex with their medals. Jane Sutherland carefully squashed the last cream-moistened crumbs of chocolate log between the prongs of her fork, wiped her soft hands carefully on the linen napkin, and picked up the print. 'May I?' She scrutinized it closely. 'Good legs.'

'You should get the girls to model swim-suits in that fashion parade you're organizing for the school,' said Mrs Allardyce.

Joyce Benton, making a final round with the coffee percolator, smiled.

---

I am Alexandra, on her best behaviour.

'And on my left,' said the chairman, who was seventy if he was a day, 'two charming young ladies who I'm sure you'll agree will wear the New Zealand silver fern in Rome most graciously — Miss Alex Archer and Miss Maggie Benton.'

Heavy words, heavy atmosphere, all these men in identical grey suits below us, such a dismal room — high, dingy-cream ceiling, embossed with all sorts of ribbons and bows and flowers, and long tired curtains in a depressing pattern of browns and greens. How could anyone *choose* such designs, such colours? After the lunch — minuscule portions of stew and two veg, custard and tinned fruit salad, served by prim girls in aprons — cigarettes and pipes were being brought out, chairs pushed back and grey legs crossed for the floor show.

Maggie and I were both wearing specially pressed school uniforms. Mum even had my blazer dry-cleaned. There wasn't much I could do about my Roman haircut, or my bloodshot eyes. At a front table below the stage sat my parents, who looked shy and out of place, and Mrs Benton, who was being most uncommonly pleasant, dressed to kill in a silk dress, pearls, crocodile handbag and a hat with a little veil.

On the other side of the chairman at the top table sat — guess who — Mr Upjohn, introduced as 'a valued Rotarian, successful manufacturer, and leading sports administrator'. I must confess to being taken aback when he strutted in the door. You didn't win your little battle, I thought, nastily, as he went through the motions of warmly congratulating Maggie and me, hoping that we would all be enjoying a trip to Rome in August, with much bonhomie and chuckles. Anyone watching would have taken him for a jovial well-loved uncle.

We heard about forthcoming meetings and played some jolly after-lunch games, which involved members being fined for assorted 'sins'. Someone walked round and rattled a wooden box, and various members tried to cap each other's jokes and everyone chuckled heartily as the sinner paid up. I had to keep reminding myself that these were the city's captains of industry, our country's leaders.

After fifteen minutes of Cyril Upjohn on the glories of sporting endeavour, the Olympic movement, the amateur ideal, and our country's youth as the hope for the future, I was beginning to think Maggie and I were there for decorative purposes only. We had, I thought, been asked to take part in a panel discussion. He spoke glowingly of our careers, our rivalry, our achievements which put us into world class, our shining examples to juniors (oh yes?!), our worthiness to go to Rome representing our country, wearing the coveted black blazer. Well, he'd been nominated as manager, if we didn't go, neither did he. Then he got on to the need for money for training camps like those being run so successfully in Australia, for trips to Australian meetings, visits by top coaches, all to raise standards. I have to admit, he was very convincing.

Almost as an afterthought, he invited questions from the floor. A thin grey figure rose from near the back.

'Could I ask our young visitors — how do they feel about facing swimmers who have the advantage of these American sports scholarships or Australian training camps you've talked about?'

Mr Upjohn turned to Maggie, who looked pointedly at me.

'Scared,' I said, raising a few chuckles. Then because no one else said anything, I said, 'Well, they're sort of professional really. I don't see much difference between being paid an actual salary to train and big prizes if you win, or having all your expenses paid for you to train and travel and everything. It's the way it's going. Unless we go the same way we'll always be at a disadvantage.'

They seemed a bit nonplussed at that. In fact, I think they were generally nonplussed by these females at the top table, instead of the usual experts giving lengthy speeches on the state of the economy. I looked down at the sea of elderly male faces (several had their eyes closed, as in sleeping — the lunch had been too much for them) and said rather lamely, 'We'll do our best.' Then another figure rose.

'Mr Upjohn, can you tell us what the selection criteria were for these charming young ladies to be nominated?'

This should be interesting.

'We look at comparative times, assessing the potential for a swimmer to make it into the Olympic final of his or her event. It was very clear that only Miss Benton and Miss Archer had that potential.'

There was a silence.

'Can I say — that wasn't an awful lot of help,' I said. 'How can you assess finalists' times with world records falling like ninepins every year? It would have been easier, not just for me and Maggie but some of the others too, if we'd been given some actual times to aim at, no matter how tough they were.'

I looked over at Maggie, whose eyes had gone all huge. There was a rustle of interest among the suits, and Mum's head was shaking to and fro slightly. But Mr Upjohn was smiling genially at the audience, making it clear he had no intention of taking me seriously. 'We are well informed on current overseas times.'

'But how can you possibly guess . . .?'

'We are not dealing in guesswork, Alex.' It was a crocodile smiling at me. 'We simply prefer not to set times,' he said, end of discussion.

Another figure rose unsteadily to his feet. 'Miss Benton, you are remarkably slight for a world-class swimmer. Why do you think you have this talent?'

Maggie blushed, not so used to performing in public as me, Sixth Form prefect, survivor of school productions and general show-off. 'I don't know really,' she said. 'I just love the water, swimming . . . I don't mind the training . . .'

'She could swim before she was two, in Singapore,' I helped her. 'She trains very hard. She's got big hands and feet like flippers. She's a great fighter, the hardest person I know to beat,' I said, warming to her praises. 'More often than not, she's won.'

'Isn't it unfeminine for young girls to partake in such strenuous and competitive sports?' said another, younger man. Well, fortyish as opposed to eightyish. Mum's eyes were glinting with warning signals, and there was an encouraging smile on the face of the Mrs Benton tiger.

'Maggie, do you think we're unfeminine?' I turned and looked at her, staring into her hands, very embarrassed. He'd got me on the raw; besides it was a rude and tasteless question in the circumstances. 'I don't feel unfeminine, unless of course you're talking about these school uniforms which aren't exactly flattering, are they? Or is it for protection?'

I looked straight at him.

'Do you think we *should* be protected from training five miles a day and going to the Olympics, for our own sakes? Like the Maoris not going to South Africa with the All Blacks next month?'

'I take it then, Miss Archer, you have strong views on the South African question . . .?'

'Yes I do, especially after Sharpeville.'

I felt another rustle, this time of disapproval. But the chairman was on his feet. 'Gentlemen, honoured guests . . . Cyril Upjohn, Miss Benton and Miss Archer, such charming and spirited young ambassadors for our country . . . our time is up.' Asked to show their appreciation of a most interesting half hour, the audience applauded politely. Then it was more bowing and scraping at the top table before Maggie and I could join our parents. If Mr Upjohn was angry he didn't show it; he was charm itself.

'Strong stuff, Alex,' said Dad. He sounded more resigned than displeased. 'Most interesting,' said a Rotary man sitting with them. 'You would seem to have considerable experience in public speaking, Alex?'

'Only in plays and stuff at school,' I said. Mrs Benton was still sitting down, looking at herself in a powder compact. Then a reporter, young, female, and eager, appeared at my elbow. 'Please, Alex, just a few more quotes, what you'd have said if the chairman hadn't closed the discussion.'

'What about?'

'The All Black team.'

'Oh, well, I only think like lots of other people. Maoris are New Zealanders, aren't they? It's supposed to be a New Zealand team. Just like we send the best possible team to the Olympics.'

She was scribbling furiously. You are getting out of your depth, Alex.

'Sorry, I have to go.' I muttered something about five a.m. training, but it was really to avoid Mr Upjohn who was heading our way. I didn't think he'd stop at ticking me off in public if he felt like it. I gathered Mum and Dad around me to make our final thanks to the chairman for lunch etcetera, and left Maggie and her mother to chat on.

Out of those few scraps, the reporter managed to cook up a small story for the next day's paper. Olympic nominee supports Maori All Blacks. 'Swimmer Alex Archer, guest at a Rotary lunch in Auckland yesterday, spoke out strongly in support of Maori players being included on the forthcoming South African tour. . .' and a few direct quotes, reasonably correct. But the last paragraph read, 'National swimming selector Mr Cyril Upjohn said that while Miss Archer's views were her own and undoubtedly sincere, he believed that competitors from one sporting code should refrain from commenting on the internal affairs of another.'

---

'This is Keith.'

Just home from training, my eyes are so sore that just to close them while I talk is a relief. 'Hi.'

'I saw that bit in the paper about you.'

'Which bit?'

'Yesterday. About the All Black thing. Want to come on the march?'

'What march?'

'Up Queen Street. The Rugby Union's dug its toes in, the Government's a pack of lily-livered cowards. Not one of them will come out and say it, *do* anything. We need people, lots of people, to march, show them.'

'Who's we?'

'Citizens All Black Tour Association — I'm a member, lots from varsity are. From what you said in the paper . . .'

'I still don't know what you're talking about.'

'Didn't you tell those Rotary creeps that you supported no Maoris, no tour?'

'Yes, but . . .'

'So you'll march? If you believed what you said, you'll march. The date isn't fixed yet. I'll let you know.'

'Now wait a minute . . .'

'It'll be a weekend, a morning. I'll come and pick you up, eight o'clock.'

'I'll still be at training.' And I'm not ever driving with you again, mate.

'Where do you train, the Tepid Pool in town?'

'Yes, but . . .'

'The march starts in Quay Street, just along from there.'

'I thought you approved of the All Blacks' going. That night at Helensville . . .'

'I did then. I don't now. What time do you finish?'

My soggy brain is beginning to wake up. I am being bullied. Into the silence he says, 'Well, if you finish by nine that'll be fine. I'll wait for you outside. Be in touch. By the way, want to come sailing?'

That wakes me up properly. He'd caught me off balance about the march and all that political stuff, but sailing with him is another matter. 'No thanks.'

'Please yourself.'

'I will.'

'That day out with Andy, he said you were great. Good feel for the boat, nice touch on the jibsheets, 'til you jumped over.'

And that silences me properly. He is grinning, I can tell.

'Are you there? Alex?'

I put the phone down slowly. How much else does he know? The reason for our fight, and me jumping over? I was a stubborn little girl, who couldn't take advice — is that what Andy told him? I was hot stuff, not bad at kissing for a beginner, responsible for one or two bruises on that manly neck — did he tell him that too? I had thought, Andy Richmond, that what went on between thee and me was private. I was wrong, it seems.

'Who was that?' asks Mum passing the phone with a pile of clothes in her arms. 'Anything wrong?'

'No. Someone from school.'

I don't like the once-over I am getting, so I stand up and try to look businesslike. 'Where's Dad? When can I have a driving lesson?'

'I thought we'd been over all that.'

'I'm fifteen and a third, and all my friends . . .'

'*All* of them?'

'Nearly all. Ninety-five per cent, with their licences *and* borrowing the car.'

'Your father and I don't approve of 15-year-old drivers. Most of your classmates are older than you. That's all there is to it.'

'But can't I *start*? I've got to learn some time.'

'When you've got fewer pressures on you.'

'That's rubbish. I'm not doing piano any more, or hockey, or ballet . . .'

'There are other pressures. And Olympics or not, you've got exams at the end of the year . . .'

I snort. 'Accrediting. No one misses accrediting except the real dummies.'

Her gaze is level and disconcerting. 'Alex, just occasionally your arrogance worries me.'

'Oh Mum . . .'

'I'm getting rather tired of you slopping round in jeans. And the state of your bedroom. It's my considered opinion that driving lessons . . .'

'Oh forget it.' I flounce up the hallway towards said bedroom, which I must admit is a bit of a mess. I intended shutting the door, but I am followed.

'I forgot — something rather more to the point. Mrs Benton rang this morning.'

'Her.'

'She was very pleasant. Said that she really didn't have a chance to congratulate you properly at the Rotary lunch.'

'What's she after?'

'You don't like her?'

'Not much.' Where would I start, mother dearest, if I was to tell you all the slights and indignities over the years? Have you forgotten what happened in Napier, only a few weeks ago? You couldn't have!

'She struck me as very sincere, said she was very pleased at the prospect of you and Maggie travelling together to Rome. Apparently she and her husband are planning to go too. They have friends there.'

'They would.'

'She's planning a surprise barbecue for Maggie's birthday, and to celebrate your nominations. Next Saturday I think, but an invitation will come in the mail. I told her I thought you'd be delighted to go.'

'Charmed.' For Maggie, yes I'll go. Because I've never actually been to Maggie's house, and I'm curious. And because no one asks me to anything much these days, except strangers with all their ghastly prize-givings and talent quests. And because I don't trust Mrs Benton one inch.

Maggie's house was grander than I'd ever dreamed, set amongst huge trees with large beds of spiky bare rose bushes. Mrs Benton grew roses, one good thing about her. I walked up the drive, with my inevitable damp hair because I'd come more or less straight from training, feeling like Cinderella without the ball gown. There was an impressive porch and inside the open door I could see lots of Chinese-looking vases and statues, blue and gold rugs and chunky black carved furniture which I supposed was also Chinese. It made my house look very homely and untidy, and Andy's house seem very proper and boring. Before I could pull the bell, Mrs Benton came trit-trotting down the staircase.

'Alex, so pleased you could come. Welcome, my dear. Maggie doesn't know a thing about it.'

'Isn't she here?'

'Her father's whisked her away to see some relatives. By the time she gets back, everyone should have arrived.'

Her eyes had quickly run down my clothes, and registered disapproval of my jeans, check shirt, floppy pullover tied around my waist, and flat shoes.

'I'm so glad you've come casually dressed, Alex,' she said, most graciously. 'For a barbecue after all.'

'That's what I thought too.' I smiled grimly, and thought if only you knew, there'd been an almighty row in the car when Dad had picked me up from the pool. He insisted on taking me home to change; I'd changed my shirt but stood my ground over jeans. Everyone will be in dresses and skirts, and the boys in ties, Mum had protested. Not me, I'm going *like this*, I hate skirts and why should I dress up for Mrs Benton — because she is your host — well I don't care, it's a barbecue and . . . go away, leave me *alone*, and Gran had put her skinny arm around my shoulder and pleaded with Mum and Dad to let me make my own decisions.

So there I was, in my jeans, shown through the house and out through French doors to a sort of courtyard with crimson bougainvilleas and pot plants all around; an uncle type decked out in a chef's hat and a rude apron standing over a sizzling barbecue, and about twenty others my age standing round with glasses of punch in their hands. The girls were dressed up to the nines, best satin cotton frocks and matching sandals, white cardigans because the air was nippy, hair set, some with pancake and eyeliner, and not one of them was more than five foot three.

Mrs Benton introduced me as if I was Maggie's best and most dearest friend, 'nominated for the Olympics too, with Maggie, you will all have heard about Alex'. I thought I was going to be sick.

'Well, well, the American, from Milwaukee,' said a plummy voice.

'American? What are you talking about, Christopher? This is Alex, Christopher Allardyce.'

'Of course. The tall and beautiful Alex, all the way from Epsom. We met at Maggie's dance, last year, didn't we?'

Oh gawd. Christopher, with a face like a turnip, with whom I'd done a travesty of a waltz at my first ever dance. Last year, last May to be precise, my childhood ago.

'Who were you with that night?' he said. 'I can't remember.'

Mrs Benton hesitated only slightly before stepping in and asking me what I would like to drink. Mercifully, someone heard a car at that point, and we all hushed, and in came Maggie and her father to much acclaim. There were more drinks and then the barbecue, which I have to admit was beautifully done, chicken and spuds done in silver foil. I managed to avoid being alone with Christopher until shortly before Dad was due to come and pick me up at nine-thirty.

He must have seen me looking at my watch, because he came sidling over at the first moment I was not quite part of a group, with what looked like a whisky in one hand and a cigarette in the other. 'The night is but young.'

'Not for me. I have to go.'

'Of course, you train at ungodly hours. How many miles a day?'

'About five.'

'Amazing.' He shook his head in mock wonder. Then he said

slyly, 'You didn't fool me, you know, Miss Milwaukee, 1959, with the yankee accent. Not for a minute.'

I looked at him straight, until his eyes dropped. 'Ah guess ah did. Otherwise you wouldn't have remembered it so-o clearly.'

He drained the whisky glass, and I felt his free hand grope for mine. I remembered that hand, damp and knobbly. I drew mine away, and said, 'Tell me, what part of England did you grow up in? Somewhere in the Cotswolds? Oxfordshire? Kent?' Where else was there, where they spoke posh?

'Cambridge? Knightsbridge? Or Hertford, Hereford and Hampshire, hurricanes hardly happen,' I said, emphasizing the Eliza haitches in 'Rain in Spain' song from *My Fair Lady*.

'I was born here, actually.'

'Oh, so you're not English, ack-chew-ally,' I said sweetly. 'Just a Kiwi like the rest of us. I could have sworn, with that B.B.C. voice . . .' Too late, he got the point, and even blushed. But I'll say this for him, he was a stayer. Or just thick. He lit another cigarette from the one already in his mouth, and said, 'Can I take you home? I should be honoured.'

'My father's coming.'

'You could ring him . . .'

'No I couldn't. He's coming at nine-fifteen. Now.'

'Another time? May I ring? Could you stretch a point and come to the pictures some time?'

Oh gawd. 'I'm not . . .'

'Someone else? Are you going steady?'

Was it any of his business? 'I don't go out at the moment. At all.'

'Such dedication. You danced so beautifully that night, in your bare feet, as I recall. Who were you with again?'

There was only one way out of this.

'Andrew Richmond. Went to Auckland Grammar, prefect, First Fifteen, rep. swimmer, stuttered, only child, a gentleman, would now be aged eighteen. He died.' I didn't stop to see how he took it. If he was embarrassed, that was his problem. Besides the whole evening had been a disaster, despite, or because of, all the toasts that Maggie's mother, warmed up with gin, had proposed to our two wonderful Olympic girls, and the birthday cake-cutting, and the presents which Maggie had been made to open there and then, with my offering looking very insignificant. A celebration? Maggie didn't look all that thrilled, Mrs Benton had been so charming and generous and nice to me it made me want to puke, and I couldn't get out quick enough. With superb timing the front door bell went just as I turned away from Christopher Allardyce so that he should not see the tears running down my face; it was Dad, firmly declining offers from Mr Benton to come in and have a drink, to the rescue.

---

The letter was written on his business paper, Cyril D. S. Upjohn and Associates, Manufacturers and Importers of Quality Men's Clothing. An Auckland address, thick quality paper, almost like parchment, a fancy italic typewriter, dated April 4, 1960.

> *Dear Alexandra,*
>
> *May I first offer my sincerest congratulations to you on your nomination for selection as a member of the New Zealand Olympic team to Rome.*
>
> *As chairman of the selection committee, I have watched your development, and that of Maggie Benton, with great interest and admiration. I'm sure you are aware that your particular achievement, against considerable odds, in winning two national titles and the recent improvement in your times contributed greatly towards our final decision to nominate you both.*
>
> *I am sure that you also recognize the responsibility that the nomination places upon you, to uphold the fine reputation of the National Swimming Association, its officials and its membership. We expect the highest standards of conduct from our leading competitors at all times, both in and out of the water.*
>
> *May I wish you continued progress with your training in these six weeks leading up to the final selection by the Olympic selectors. As the nominated manager, I look forward with confidence to our joint selection and the resulting pleasure of accompanying you and Maggie to the Rome Olympiad in August.*
>
> *Sincerely yours,*

And signed in an unintelligible scrawl, Cyril Upjohn.
I'm glad that some instinct (survival?) that Saturday had led

me to check the mailbox as soon as I heard the postie's whistle. No one knows of the official-looking envelope addressed to me which now lies on my bed, while I stare at the letter and see it for what it is: a warning.

Keep your head down, Miss Alex.

Nothing political. No asking the selectors awkward questions in public. No rudeness to reporters or ill-informed comments about the All Black team or rumours about bad behaviour at school. Thou shalt be grateful and graceful in all thy public and private doings, otherwise thou shalt not be going to Rome.

It is not inconceivable that a nomination be withdrawn, or even a selection.

Between the lines, that's the message to little girls. The man can't stand tall women. He doesn't want me in Rome. He had to select me because I made it impossible for him not to, but he's going to make me pay the price of coming into line.

I tear the letter into little shreds. Then I take them out to the incinerator and burn them. Then I surprise Gran by offering to clean out the chooks' cage because hens are creatures of peace, and soothing to stroke, and because there no one can see my fury.

I stand stunned in the hallway from another late-night phone call, looking stupidly at the telephone in my hand.

My last anchor has gone. Now I'm completely adrift, without direction, in a sea of people who all want something from me I can't give. I don't know anything anymore, how to behave, what to say, how to react; even, or especially, the common courtesies at home, at school; all seem hollow and meaningless or sinister and threatening; everywhere in my life but with you, my anchor at the pool because you ask nothing of me except that I immerse myself in water and blank out my mind . . . become an automaton . . . and swim.

'I'll write, Alex,' Mr Jack said, 'or cable, soon as I can, and let you know when I'm coming back.'

And now he's gone, too, like all the rest in one way or another. Gone hurriedly to Australia because his old mother in Sydney who's had emphysema for some years has suddenly got worse, and he's flying out tomorrow morning on the first Electra flight from Whenuapai.

'I couldn't get much sense out of my sister when she rang,' he said, 'except that it's bad. I might be only a week, or several.'

Please don't go, I am yelling silently, I need you. I have five weeks' training before the final Olympic selections, and two sets of time trials and short-course record attempts scheduled to convince the overall selectors, if they still need convincing, that I'm not resting on my laurels — I need you.

The reality of my nomination — because, whatever else, I have the cutting from the newspaper pinned up beside my bed to reassure myself at five o'clock every morning that it's true — and you standing on the side of the pool as I plough up and down — those are the only things I know are real any more.

He would write out my schedules on the plane, and put them in the post. I'd like to have come over and seen you before I go, he said, but I've run out of time. He'd talk to my Dad, give him the low-down; since Dad still came with me in the mornings, he could take my times, and I had my log book right up to date, didn't I?

The afternoons — he'd thought of asking Maggie's coach to take me on — no thanks, I said — but decided to ask Steve, one of the younger coaches from another pool who didn't have any people still training. Was I happy with all that?

Happy? About to be cast adrift? Sure, I whimpered. You know Steve, don't you, Alex? He's good with his kids. And he lives pretty near you. Finishes work at four, so he's happy to give you a lift there and back.

He's not you, I thought.

'You've got about five weeks before the final selection. I'm sure I'll be back long before that. And we should have some official time trials in about three weeks.'

'Suppose.'

'Alex, I know this isn't easy for you. But you don't need anyone to crack a whip over you. I know that.'

'Please . . . don't be too long. I hope your mother's OK.'

'Thanks champ. T.T.F.N.'

'Ta ta, just for now,' I said sadly. It's the next morning, on the way to the pool that I begin to cry. In the dark, the rain beating on the windscreen, the car sluicing its way through great puddles caused by drains blocked with dead leaves, I turn my head away, pretending to doze off, and Dad doesn't notice. The pool, without the squat body planted on the bench with stop-watch, thermos of tea and morning *Herald*, seems an echoing treacherous space of nothing.

---

April passes in a haze of sore eyes, twice daily at those terrible baths, school in between. I'm a robot. Dad times my morning stuff, and Steve the after school session. We get word from Mr Jack that his mother is still hanging on — it turns out to be not quite as bad as they thought, not bad enough to carry her off, but she's on oxygen and can't last much longer. His voice on the long-distance call, at least what we can hear of it through the crackles, is flat and tired. The days, the weeks, drag by. Maggie does her stints on the other side of the pool, her mother continues to be pleasant. I am still wary.

Steve's OK, at first. He used to be a swimmer too, now has a young squad, not actually training at the moment because it's the winter lay-off period, two kids of his own, and a beer belly. He works peculiar shifts as a printer somewhere, so he picks me up from school and we go straight to the pool. We have Mr Jack's handwritten notes for each week's schedule.

About the third week of April I come in for some tongue-lashing.

'Next time, get your skates on, Alex. That wasn't good enough,' he says looking at the stop-watch as though it was going to bite him. I sit on the side of the pool with my chest heaving and my eyes out on red-hot stalks, knowing I have still another four 100 metre sprints at two minute intervals not to mention the ten one-lap sprints at thirty second intervals, and I hate his very guts. The next time it happens, though I know he is right, I shout back, with tears of rage in my eyes.

'Come on, Alex, put some ginger into it,' he says in tones of deep disgust. 'That's a pathetic effort. You're not trying.'

'I am bloody trying, leave me alone,' I shout, and storm into the dressing room, and refuse to get back in the pool or say one single word to him on the way home.

For a few days we get by. Then I notice the distances have gone up. I ask to see the schedules, he tries to distract me, I insist, and see that what he is telling me to do and what is written there by Mr Jack are two quite different things.

'You need more mileage, the Aussie girls are doing twice as much,' he says.

'They're not doing ten miles a day.'

'They're up to forty miles a week.'

'I'm doing five a day, seven times a week, thirty-five miles, exactly as I was told.'

'You're slacking, Alex. Afraid to push yourself just that bit extra?'

'I'm doing Mr Jack's schedule. Not yours. He's still my coach, whatever you might think.' I walk off, swearing softly, which I think he hears, dive in and complete the session. When I get out he has gone, telling the receptionist in the office that he never wants to set eyes on that bumptious kid Alex Archer again, and because I haven't any money on me to get a bus home I have to ring Dad at work, which is something only done in emergencies, and ask him to come and get me.

Even before we get home, Steve's been on the phone to Mum, saying he's had enough of my lip and can't cope with me any more, Olympic prospect or not, and good luck to her because I'm a sullen young lady with a few problems, and he's not surprised she's got a reputation for insolence and general bad behaviour, he only took her on because Bill Jack's a good friend, but he doesn't know how he's kept her in his squad all these years, and if she was my daughter she'd be in for a good hiding if she spoke to adults like that.

I know all this because Mum is so upset when we arrive home that she's not in the kitchen cooking tea but in her bedroom, and they forget to close the door before she pours it all out on Dad's shoulder. It's not that I am eavesdropping, I can just hear her voice and her crying all over the house. Gran gives the subdued kids their tea, I lock myself in my bedroom, and refuse to even answer Dad when he knocks. I have never, ever, seen Mum cry before, except pleased tears when I won something, and I don't ever want to again. I cry myself to sleep; I've given up everything, lost everything, lost everyone. For what?

When my alarm goes off at five a.m. the next morning, I can still hear Mum's crying in my head. Almost immediately, someone knocks on the door. 'Alex? We going?' 'Yes.' Somehow I manage to get vertical; I have to keep going, whatever happens, if I stop now I might never start again, Dad knows that, which is why he's up and ready to go, as per normal. I didn't clean my teeth last night. Ten minutes later we're driving through the dark. Dad doesn't say a single word about Mum or Steve. He doesn't need to.

So much for Steve. Dad now takes me twice daily, but we can't go until he finishes work at five, and we don't get home until nearly eight, by which time my eyes feel like they've been boiled in oil and I can do nothing more, after dinner, than crawl into bed and dread the ring of the alarm the next morning.

Two days after Steve threw in the sponge, Mr Jack rings and says his mother is on her last legs, they don't expect her to last the week, and how am I getting on? I suppress a strong desire to let fly, but what's the use? He can't come home anyway. I don't tell him about Steve. Everything's fine, I say, looking good for the time trials soon, I'm beginning to taper off, feeling good, feeling great. I'm a good liar.

---

There was one tiny pleasure that awful April, one only. A few days after we started reading *Saint Joan*, Miss Macrae called me to stay behind after class. I stayed in my seat, because I was barely awake after another dreary lesson spent bashing all the life out of George Bernard Shaw; the scene with Joan and the Dauphin at court. She planted her bulky backside on a nearby desk, and straightened the pleats in her grey skirt. She was not usually so ponderous, intimidating. Her voice, when she began, was curiously non-committal.

'I'm planning the production at the end of the year. For a change, I thought a Shaw evening — a scene from *Pygmalion*, some songs from *My Fair Lady*, an extract perhaps from *Caesar and Cleopatra*. There are too many male parts, and not enough talent for the whole of *Saint Joan*, but we can do excerpts, possibly three scenes.'

I shrugged. So? I may or may not be away in Rome for five weeks, and anyway she hadn't given me the chance to read Joan. It hardly concerned me.

'When do you know about Rome?' she said.

'Middle of May.'

'If you go to Rome, when is it?'

'About August 10, the games start August 25, the team comes home about September 20.' I realized, by rattling off the dates, I was betraying how much it meant to me.

'School holidays would account for three weeks of that. Well, it's just possible.'

'What is?'

'I'll put my cards on the table, Alex. Even if you go to Rome, with all the attendant disruption and excitement — could you manage between now and November to learn and rehearse three scenes?'

'What as?'

She looked at me in surprise. 'Joan.'

'Kathie's been reading it.'

'And badly. Painful for you, who could do it so much better. Excruciating for me, who has performed the role. Behind the don't-care leave-me-alone mask you are wearing these days, you were angry. Yes? I was relieved you still have some ambitions besides cutting minuscule slices off your swimming times.'

I shrugged again, hardly wanting her to know that she was right. Joan! Who said what she thought and obeyed her voices, lived briefly and gloriously and in the end got dragged off to die the way I sometimes wished someone would do to me.

'Think about it, Alex. Let me know next week. You might want to talk it over with your parents.'

I've stopped talking to them too, I thought, and they've stopped listening and anyway who in her right mind would refuse Joan.

'I know you're being particularly single-minded at present, for the first time in your life. I also believe that despite what you and most other people might think, you're still deeply grieving for your soulmate Andrew, at odds with yourself and everyone.'

I could only look out of the window. My soulmate. Grieving

— is this what grieving feels like? I'm not wearing black and weeping and wailing all over the place as they do in films, but my eyes were suddenly full of tears. A fake cough to stop them dripping down my cheeks didn't fool Miss Macrae for one minute.

'I think you're punishing yourself. Physically, mentally. Drowning yourself in water and pain. And another thing — why so long until the final selection of the Olympic team? This has been going on for months.'

'I don't know. It might have something to do with being in the wrong hemisphere, out of season.'

'I simply don't understand. To keep people in hard training, for so long — there's a lack of compassion somewhere. It'd be like having to learn the whole of Hamlet just for an audition, and seeing someone else chosen.'

She realized her lack of tact.

'You know what I mean. The papers keep saying you should be selected for Rome. Will be. Well, for the sake of your health, you've got to start thinking positively, *now*, about something other than a stop-watch.'

She stood up. 'Joan is a real challenge, believe you me. Think about it.'

I read the play again in class, while we were supposed to be doing a Latin prose. Even if it was only three scenes, it was a gift, a treasure, a plum of a part! I would probably never get the chance again. Joan had no time for pompous officials, she said what she thought and she wore what she pleased, and she did what her conscience and her passion and her ambition told her. And I realized, as I read on through break, and into History, that there had been something missing besides a social life, or a home life or anything other than a swimming life. I must have got very boring.

---

Unexpected visitors always annoyed Joyce Benton. She was used to the politer ways of the English country life of her childhood, where one normally first called by telephone to arrange a visit; or Singapore where the amah was trained to provide minimal hospitality to unannounced or unwelcome visitors until she was ready to appear. Here, women frequently popped in and out of each other's houses. Joyce Benton had made her dislike of the practice clear when she first came to live in Auckland. Now she was rarely disturbed during the hours when Maggie and Isobel were away at school, the quiet hours she filled with running her large house, supervising the housekeeper and gardener who came twice a week, and organizing the dinner parties demanded of her by her husband's business interests.

She had been hoping for this visit, however, and though given no warning, welcomed it. She put Jane Sutherland into a deep chair with a copy of Vogue and went out to the kitchen to make some coffee. Her tins were full of yesterday's baking; she deliberately selected chocolate iced afghans, cheese fingers; the most fattening.

'I hope you don't mind me popping in,' said Jane Sutherland, still perched on the edge of the armchair.

'Not at all.'

'I wanted to check with you first, before I ask Maggie.'

'Oh? Ask her what?'

'Well, some mothers might . . . your cheese fingers are superb, Joyce.'

'Thank you.' Joyce Benton waited patiently. Her guest had a laddered stocking, and no self-discipline when it came to food; if she wanted to get into the fashion game, thought Joyce Benton, Jane would have to make sure her city smart appearance went deeper than the expensive suit. It was the details she needed to attend to. And lose about a stone and a half.

'I had this phone call the other day. You know the girls who do dressmaking at school, making outfits for the parade in July? My daughter's doing so well. Well. Right out of the blue, I've been offered some of the new season's swim-suits. The 1961 California season, imagine that! They'd heard that our school's show was a little bit special. And I thought . . .'

Joyce Benton sipped her coffee. She was not going to be seen to enthuse.

'I thought, two wonderful young swimmers, wouldn't it be tremendous? Two Olympic models. We can make it a charity event, raise money for the Crippled Children or something.'

'You mean, you see Maggie as a model?'

'And Alex Archer. That photo I saw when I came for coffee — such fine girls, both of them, wonderful figures. I know Alex goes to that other school, but I'm sure, if it's for charity . . .'

Joyce Benton offered her animated guest more coffee, presenting a reaction of coolness, even reluctance.

'I don't know, Jane. Maggie's very young. Won't these all be very sophisticated garments?'

'Oh, but beautiful. I've seen them, Grecian styles, very classical, with little skirts, and South Sea Isle prints, the South Pacific look, big flowers, you know, gorgeous colours, even some with matching beach coats.'

'They sound lovely.'

'Oh, they are. And I'd just love to have Maggie and Alex . . .' Jane Sutherland was disconcerted by the lack of response. 'It's only a school thing, just the girls and a few parents. Perhaps you're worried about the time involved?'

'Not so much that.'

'Only one or two rehearsals, just to make sure the swim-suits fit and the girls know what to do?'

After a brief pause, Joyce Benton said, 'Let me discuss it with Maggie. After all, she is the one who's got to do it. More coffee?'

'Of course, naturally. Oh, yes please.' She held out her cup. 'I did enjoy your coffee morning the other week. How long before the final selection? How are the girls coping?'

'About three weeks. Maggie is coping very well, I feel. Alex, I'm not sure; she's looking very strained these days, losing weight. She was here for a barbecue recently, and didn't seem to fit in terribly well, though of course we did all we could . . . I do worry about the child.'

She got up to close a window. 'It's getting chilly, these days. I rather dread the winter, the incessant rain, the damp of this climate. Perhaps . . . leave it a while, your suggestion. After the selections are announced, maybe?'

'I'll have to let the man from the department store know.'

Oh, he'll wait, thought Joyce Benton. I only know George Sadler through Harold's business contacts, but it had been relatively simple to include him and his dreary wife in a recent cocktail party. He'll wait, because even 'a school thing' is good promotion for him; and it had been difficult to restrain him from the idea of mounting a whole fashion parade in his genteel but slightly shabby department store around the idea of Olympic models; quite against the amateur code, I had to explain, but maybe a school parade, no one could object to that. Incidentally, George, depite her rather flamboyant appearance, Jane Sutherland is still a rather . . . insecure little person, not very experienced. This is her first parade for the school. Her husband is rather a difficult man. Say that you'd heard the emphasis the school put on good grooming and dressmaking, and about their excellent annual parade. Let her think it was her idea.

'Delighted to see you. Thank you so much for calling,' she said coolly as she saw her guest to her car in the brick driveway. 'I'll be in touch.'

---

We swam into winter, into May, two weeks to go. Mr Jack was still away in Sydney, Dad faithfully clocking my time trials, the household ticking away as usual, though I saw precious little of anyone.

Maggie and I survived two official time trials, 100 metres and 400 metres; unofficial sprint records for us both but not allowable because they were done in a short-course salt water pool. The first time, I had the faster time by point one; the second time, Maggie did, by the same margin, but not enough to tip the balance in her favour. So I still had the edge; and Mrs Benton was still going out of her way to be charming when I let her get anywhere near me. We got small bits in the paper, about our heavy training schedules and these unofficial records 'reinforcing our claims for two places in the Games team', and 'keeping the pressure on the Olympic selectors'.

I'd lost another five pounds and my hip bones were sticking out.

The papers were full of the all-white All Blacks soon to leave for South Africa despite the petitions and general public outcry. I hadn't forgotten Keith's suggestion about the protest march, but I was simply too tired, and my eyes too sore to do anything except wait for him to ring back. Training, sitting in class, and using lunch-times and what free periods I had to read *Saint Joan* over and over — my life had come down to this.

Keith rang the night before the march, with only a week to go before the Olympic team was due to be announced. He was abrupt to the point of rudeness.

'Alex? You a starter? Nine o'clock tomorrow, outside the pool, OK, gotta go, seeya,' again leaving me holding the phone in amazement.

Sure enough, outside the pool there he was. For some reason of native cunning I hadn't told my parents what I was doing after training, other than 'meeting some friends, going to an eleven o'clock film in town'. Life had got so dull, they seemed to think *South Pacific* and the new wonders of the big screen were a good idea for a Saturday morning.

'What's wrong with your eyes?' I was beginning to find out Keith didn't waste time on the usual courtesies, like hullo, how are you, and goodbye. I hadn't been quite quick enough with my sunglasses.

'It's the water. Salt and chlorine mixed, then heated.'

'What about goggles?'

'I can't keep them on. The suction, it's like pulling out your eyeballs.'

'Christ.'

I looked a bit funny in sunglasses, 'cause it was overcast and wintry. Coming with wet hair from the fug of a heated pool, I was envious of the marchers who'd dressed warmly in hats, warm coats, gloves and handknitted scarves about nine feet long. Keith seemed to know lots of the students in duffle coats. We milled around a bit with families, vicars in dog collars, students; and Maoris, as you might expect, 'cause it was them, who were being left out of the team 'in their best interests,' who'd been insulted. The team was due to leave the next day.

Next to me as we assembled were two men wearing New Zealand blazers — Athletics, Olympic Games, Melbourne 1956. Keith, darting round, stopped briefly to shake their hands. 'Good-ta-seeya, mate,' almost as though he had some sort of status as an organizer. Then he grabbed my hand and led me almost to the head of the parade. I ungrabbed it, and without speaking slunk back a few rows. I was here, wasn't I? That was enough. There were times when I was conscious of my tallness, and this was one of them. I didn't want to be conspicuously here. We moved off slowly.

It's the first time I've been in a large moving crowd of people since last May, the day we walked over the harbour bridge and talked of Kipling and dying. As we approach the Ferry Buildings I see a blue Morris Minor parked on the far side of the road, and leaning against it, his arms folded, watching the parade, is Andy.

I'm swept on. It's the clothes that tell me I must be wrong — he would never have worn that scruffy jacket. But the height is the same, and the hair, and the relaxed folded arms, and the smile, and so is the voice that calls my name. I'm swept past, and in my hand my sunglasses are shaking and it's not because I'm cold.

The march went past the Central Post Office, up Queen Street lined with spectators who'd come to watch. The papers said later there were 2000 marchers and 3000 spectators. Ahead of us I could hear an African drum, and people were holding banners saying 'No Maoris, No Tour' and 'Sharpeville 128-0,' 'I'm All White, Jack' and 'We want no part of Apartheid.'

We'd just turned into Queen Street, when Keith remembered he had his own banner in his duffle bag. It was a long piece of cloth, with '1960 All Blacks the Shame of New Zealand' written in crude black paint. 'Here, hold one end of this,' he said.

'No.'

'Why not?'

'I don't want to. I'm here, I'm marching, and that's all I'm doing.'

'Women,' he said. 'Here, mate, take this,' he shouted across to an older man abreast of us. I may as well have carried the damn thing, because now I was walking directly behind it.

'You're a weirdo, Alex. You'll get up at a Rotary do in public and say your piece . . . even argue with Andy's cantankerous old man.'

'How did you know about that?'

'Well, it's obvious isn't it? We were . . . mates.'

'I can't imagine why.' That hurt; he drew breath to say something, then seemed to change his mind. 'Anyway, I don't want to talk about it.'

'You're still . . .?'

'Bitter and twisted? Of course I am. Maniacs behind wheels of cars — good people die and others get away with murder. What sort of logic is that? They didn't even find the guy who did it.'

'Yes they . . .' He looked at me over his end of the banner. 'Oh Christ, Alex, didn't you know?'

'Know what? I didn't make a point of finding out, no.'

It was more than that. I'd told my family, Julia, Mr Jack that I didn't want to know, anything more about who, or why, or what happened. There'd been a brief bit about a 'hit-and-run accident in Epsom last night, 17-year-old boy killed', and I'd not looked at the newspapers for weeks after that.

'They know who did it all right, except they think he's in Australia.'

Coming on top of what I'd just seen, or not seen, I was feeling sick to the very depths. And from those depths a mighty fury was beginning to stir.

'Oh, *great*. Scot-free.'

'Him, yes. After a fashion. His wife, no.'

'How?'

'It was her that rushed out, found him . . . dying. Neighbours too, 'cause of the noise, her screaming, and before that the row in the house, him drunk as a skunk, yelling and throwing things.'

'Keep politics out of sport!' yelled a voice, penetrating. I was under a street light, a dying boy in my arms.

'The guy worked in cars. So he knocked up a friendly panel-beater in the middle of the night, and had the car locked away in a garage half way down Great South Road. Paint job, number plates, the lot. The police found it eventually. They found paint chips, on his . . .'

'Don't!!'

'They think our friend crept back to the house that night, whipped up his passport and a few clothes and shot through to Aussie. His wife couldn't, or wouldn't, tell them anything.'

'She's protecting him? Knowing he's killed someone?'

'She's not obliged to tell the police anything. Or testify if they ever did get him to court, which they won't. There were no witnesses.'

'If they did? How do you know all this?'

'My mum works for a lawyer. The secretaries, well you know what this place is like, one of them knows the wife through kindergarten. Apparently she's gone to pieces a bit.'

'*If they did?*'

'Oh, manslaughter, drunken driving, failing to stop at an accident — be put away for a few years. Could you blame the wife, she's lost a husband, big house. Three young kids to support. And he's stuck in Aussie, can't come back, lost his job, his family ... one drink too many ...'

'One little mistake? Is that what you were going to say. Did he lose *his* life? You feel sorry for *him*?'

'Go back to school, little girl,' came a voice. 'The rest of you, go back to your pulpits.'

Poofters!

Traitors!

Cranks!

'Shame,' came a few softer voices of reason from the crowd, women's voices. 'Shame.'

'Keep politics out of sport!'

'You're a pack of girls!'

'Girls don't start wars,' I yelled. 'Or kill people with cars. And they've got too much sense to play rugby, with the Springboks or anybody else.'

There was some laughter, ironic cheers. A few people clapped. I saw Keith's expression change from worry to slight amusement.

'Go back to your kitchen, girlie,' came the same voice, but fainter, now behind us. Keith was looking at me. 'Alex, I ...'

'Drop dead,' I said. We marched on through friendlier territory. Most of the crowd seemed quite amused by the whole thing, as though they were watching the Santa Parade. We had marched on up the gradual incline of Queen Street before I could bring myself to speak again.

'You're all the same. In the end. You drive like a maniac, you've had accidents, plural, and damn near killed someone, but you close ranks, you're all the same. I suppose you're going to tell me poor bastard, wife playing around and mother-in-law and three snotty kids driving him mad, so somehow you can understand a guy blowing a fuse and firing up his Jaguar ...'

Now I know why I want to do law.'

'Alex, I'm sorry. I shouldn't have told you.'

'Well you did.'

'I thought . . .'

'Forget it.' I don't know why I went on marching, why I didn't just duck off out the side and catch a bus home. Perhaps I was just shell-shocked, all the old wounds opening up. Andy would have marched, we would have marched together, I know we would have. I had to go on. So we marched in silence to the bang of the African drum up the long straight road, ending up in a kid's playground, standing around among the swings and slides listening to lengthy speeches by church leaders, Maori leaders, union leaders, men in hats. After a while they began to get rather repetitive and boring. Keith had wandered off to talk to other people; I had sunk into a sort of apathetic daze, chilled to the marrow, sitting on a roundabout. I didn't see the press photographer until his flash had gone off and it was too late.

You *fixed* that, didn't you!'

'Christ, Alex, how . . .'

'You hauled me along for a bit of cheesecake, female support, Alex Archer on behalf of New Zealand's young sportswomen standing up and being counted. You tried to get me up in front of the parade, and to carry that bloody banner, and when you couldn't you fixed the photographer.'

'I swear to God I had nothing to . . .'

'You expect me to believe that, Keith Jameson?' I yelled down the phone. 'The Olympic team gets announced in a week. Because of you . . .' I choked.

The front page of the evening paper was shaking in my hand. What was making me especially angry was the posed sort of way I was sitting, without knowing it. With damp hair, sunglasses, I looked like some sort of outsize, sulky, brooding Grace Kelly. 'Olympic nominee, swimmer Alex Archer was among the marchers'.

'Someone must have told them. How did they know it was me?'

'Come on, a face as famous as yours? Cover girl of the *Women's Weekly*?'

'I was wearing sunglasses. I was just one of thousands.'

'And you thought you were incognito? Grow up, Alex. Press photographers have memories. And they know a pretty face when they see one. All those dour Presbyterians, scruffy varsity students — can you blame them picking you out?'

'That's exactly what . . . you didn't ask me to march because I believed in it. You asked me just to get extra publicity for the cause. Cheesecake, using models to sell, draped all over cars . . . you used me, Keith Jameson and I'll never forgive you.'

'Keep your hair on, woman.'

I saw Jamie's shadow against his bedroom door. Indeed the whole house had gone remarkably quiet as they all listened from behind doorways.

'Don't you woman me.' I have yet to run the gamut of my family, or Mr Jack when he comes back and finds out I've blown it, or Mr Upjohn who may now have found the weapon he needs to inform the main selectors that I am politically unreliable and a bad influence on juniors.

'What's the matter with you anyway?' said Keith. 'Aren't you proud to be a leader? In twenty years' time no one will be going to South Africa to play *anything*, unless they change their appalling race laws. Ten years even, Olympics, rugby, trade, nothing, because of us, because of what we did yesterday. Talking and petitions aren't enough any more, we have to get out there. Protest, march, obstruct, get in the papers, make a nuisance of ourselves so that the politicians have to listen.'

'In twenty years' time I'll be looking back and thinking about the Olympic trip I missed out on.'

'Calm down, Alex. Are you seriously trying to tell me that one picture in the paper will ruin your chances? I don't believe it. This is 1960, not Orwell's 1984. You're entitled to your views . . .'

'Not if you're fifteen and female and you know damn well one selector has already got it in for you.'

'He's only one of how many, three?'

'If you *knew*, if you had any idea at all, what it's cost me to get this far . . .'

'I know one thing, Miss Alexandra Archer, and that is you've got a very high opinion of yourself. So what if your picture's in the paper doing something worthwhile, standing up against tyranny. Better than winning a swimming race, better than any medal. Andy knew that. Wouldn't he have been proud of you?'

'Don't you ever EVER say that name to me again.' I slammed down the phone, so hard that I probably cracked the casing. Gran was the first person to appear from the kitchen, wiping her hands on a tea-towel.

'I'll say it, Alex,' she said quietly, 'because you'll take it from me. Andy is proud of you, so are we all.'

'I won't get in the team, Gran,' I wept, sinking to a heap against the hallway skirtings. 'I won't, I won't, I won't.'

Everyone's abandoned me — Mr Jack's gone, Mum and Dad are pussyfooting and not talking to me, Julia's gone off with someone else, Keith is a bastard, and Andy who told me I'd be going to Rome — the unkindest cut of all.

Gran stroked my hair for a long time, wet as always because I'd only just come in from evening training when I saw the paper. The kids crept about as though someone was sick, the peas burned, and Mum stayed safely in the laundry doing the ironing.

'You'll be there.'

---

The next day Keith, along with about twenty-five others, rushes out on the tarmac at Whenuapai and flings himself down on the runway in front of the plane carrying the all white All Blacks. Earlier there was a bomb scare and the luggage was examined, and the captain led his team out after all the ordinary passengers singing 'Now is the Hour' which shows what total hypocrites they all are because they can sing a Maori song when they've left the Maoris behind. Because the Electra turns around and takes off extra quick, almost as though the crew knew what was planned, the protesters are too late to actually stop it, although the nearest gets within twenty yards, and they are left standing shaking their fists at the sky. I know about this because it's in the paper, and there he is, duffle coat awry, scarf trailing, legs planted wide in the grass, caught shouting and gesticulating, gnomish face scowling in frustration; and by then I've calmed down enough to see the funny side. See how you like *your* picture in the paper, Keith Jameson.

Mum and Dad must have decided I'd punished myself enough, because nothing is said about the cheesecake photo or even about me going protesting instead of to see *South Pacific*. An uneasy truce reigns in the house.

Maggie and I plough silently up and down the pool and exchange small talk when we meet in the dressing room, groping around for our clothes, blinded by chlorine, pink as lobsters. The days tick by, five to go, four. The team is being announced on May 25, the papers are full of the earthquakes and tidal waves in Chile, 1500 dead and 30,000 homeless, and the tsunami which is rushing across the Pacific towards our small defenceless country. People actually go down to the water's edge of the waterfront to watch it coming in, never mind getting on to higher ground. What they see is the lowest tide ever, a sea of mud stretching half-way to Rangitoto, before a fizzer of a high tide. Tsunami are too close to my nightmares in the few minutes of sleep I manage each night. The dreaded dream is back: going sailing with Andy, at first laughing and happy, but he is still jumping over the side never to surface and I'm still left to sail on alone.

It's school holidays, not that it makes much difference except that I can go training at six in the morning instead of five. Maggie, by some unspoken agreement, goes later in the day to both sessions, so that we avoid each other entirely. At home you could cut the atmosphere with a knife.

On the twenty-fifth of May I sleep in, a long, unusually dreamless sleep until after eight, which is late for me. Last night's paper has told us that the team is expected to be announced midday today: I have four hours to fill in. I can't hang around the house listening to the kids fight. A bike ride seems to be in order, and I have a score to settle.

It's only when I'm riding towards Andy's school that I realize I don't know exactly which house and which driveway it was that the Jaguar screamed out of that December night.

I haven't got any money on me for a phone box, so I go into a dairy which I know to be one of those friendly places where Mum cashes cheques every now and then. I persuade the man behind the counter to let me use his phone; I ring Keith's number.

He's not at home, of course, he's working down on the wharves during his holidays, earning vast sums of money, and his mother works too.

I know the general area, where it happened. One driveway has a large For Sale notice beside it. This would be a logical conclusion to the story I heard from Keith: the man fled to Aussie, the woman and her children gone to ground. Some ghoulish instinct has me searching for bloodstains on the road outside, but there's been a lot of sun and a lot of rain since that December night. Another instinct has me looking around to see that I am not watched, and pedalling myself slowly up the driveway, which is strewn with leaves driven into decaying piles and fallen branches. The trees and bushes are out of control, the flower beds gone to seed. It's an expensive house, the sort usually described as gracious, but empty. Broken toys in a scruffy sandpit, cardboard boxes lying round, a broken chair by the front door, evidence of the house being left in a hurry and with no thought for the next people. I walk along the porch. Except for a few boxes of rubbish, the rooms inside are empty. The garage door is shut, but being so tall I can see in through a small high window. Inside is a dark green car. Even though I can't see all of it, I know it's a Jaguar.

Perhaps it's just as well I can't see its bonnet, the sleek and dangerous sharp end that had killed him, because I think I might have lost all control of my temper, my senses, my self. I lose enough control of my temper to try to pull off the padlock that opens the side door of the garage. It's too strong; what I thought I might have done to the Jaguar had I been able to get my hands on it, I don't know. As it is, I have to let go a cry of despair that echoes round the courtyard. I have just enough control to know that neighbours might come to investigate; but not enough to stop myself picking up a large rock from the ornamental rockery in front of the house and hurling it at the side of the garage, too badly aimed to break the window; not enough to stop myself repeating the performance, twice more; enough awareness to be relieved that I am too angry to aim properly to alert neighbours to a sound of breaking glass; enough momentum to leap on my bike and free-wheel down the drive; enough sense to slow up at the bottom because the irony of me being knocked off my bike in the very spot would be too much; not enough control to go pedalling off down the road far too fast, considering I cannot see a thing for tears.

The score is not settled. What had I wanted, anyway? — to talk to the wife, feel sorry for the kids, recognize a blood stain on the road. I don't know, don't know. You told me, Andy, I was going to Rome. Was it just a weak man talking, telling me what I wanted to hear. Is Keith right when he says you wouldn't have made it to command a ship because you lacked drive, aggression, grit, you were too soft; things had come too easy for you? Have all these months been wasted? I'm up against forces I don't understand. Have you betrayed me? Did you know all the time I wouldn't get in?

Where have you gone?

While I am eating bacon and eggs for brunch, waiting for the midday news that will probably include the team, something happens in my head and I find myself telling Mum and Gran about Mr Upjohn and what I had overheard in Napier. 'I don't want her in Rome.' They look at each other, sort of helplessly.

'Why didn't you tell us earlier?'

'I don't know, Mum. I just couldn't.'

'Why?' persists Mum. 'Three months you've been soldiering on, and God knows that's not been the only problem. Why didn't you tell us at the time? Couldn't we have helped?'

'I don't know. I don't know. I don't know anything any more.'

I am crying, again, even before I hear I haven't made it into the team.

'Alex,' says Mum sternly. 'If you get in the team, no one will be prouder than your family, and no one knows better than us how hard you've worked for it. If you don't . . .'

'That'll be it,' I say. 'I'll stop as of today, training, swimming, for good.'

'I was going to say, whatever, we'll be just as proud for what you've achieved already. The greater achievement is sometimes to reassess goals.'

'She will make it, Helena,' said Gran testily, looking at the kitchen clock. It's five minutes before high noon. 'Shall I get the kids in from the garden?'

'No.' They both know I'd rather hear the worst without an

audience. Mum turns on the radio and we sit, Mum on one side, Gran on the other. Is this how a prisoner in the dock feels when the foreman reads out the verdict?

The fruity male voice drones on, events in Chile, South Africa, the Summit conference breaks down in Paris.

And then. 'Thirty-nine athletes and twelve officials have today been named for the Olympic Games to be held in Rome in August. They are ..' The announcer reads the list slowly, deliberately: the athletes, the cyclists, the equestrians, the fencers, the hockey players, is there no end to it?

The rowers, then 'Swimming. Manager, Mr Cyril Upjohn, of Auckland. Chaperon, Mrs Enid Churchill, of Christchurch.'

Someone is going. A female is going.

'Miss Alexandra Beatrice Archer, of Auckland. 100 metres and 400 metres freestyle. Miss Margaret Louise Benton, 100 metres and 400 metres freestyle. Weightlifting ..'

Like an old-fashioned heroine, I swoon.

*Part Three*

IT was a busy day for the Sports Desk, and Norm Thompson, clocking in only ten minutes late. As the Olympic team came clattering off the teleprinter machine at noon, the Sports Editor ticked off a list of interviews and pictures he wanted done that afternoon for tomorrow morning's paper. The announcement had happily come over too late for the evening paper, except for a tiny stop press in the final edition, so he expected plenty of space, on both the front page and an inside sports page.

'Murray Halberg and coach, and Peter Snell who's crept in the back door. The lady shot-putter, we've got her on file already. We need a bit of glamour . . . get the two girl swimmers together, Norm. Not a bad list, I suppose, no real surprises.'

Norm Thompson grunted, unimpressed with this off-the-cuff analysis. He was greatly relieved that justice and common sense had prevailed in the case of the two girls. It was not impossible that Alex could have missed out. The promising young butterfly swimmer hadn't made it; neither had the female runner whose half-mile times placed her among the world's top ten. Hardly a Games team had gone by without controversy, inexplicable omissions; the workings of selectors' minds remained a total mystery. He had some experience of the sort of despair and disillusionment the female half-miler would be feeling, years of work for nothing. Fortunately another reporter was being assigned to that interview, to probe and document her anguish for the nation's breakfast reading.

'You could get the cadet to go out to see young Archer and Benton. Attractive kids, he'd like that.' The Sports Editor looked at Norm across his ash-scattered paper-strewn shambles of a desk.

The cadet, thought Norm, was a lecherous little creep, if his behaviour with the copy typists around the news-room was anything to go by. He wouldn't wish that on young Archer and Benton. Besides, since her triumph at the nationals in Napier and her political notoriety of the past three months, he was curious about young Archer. In the light of what he'd heard from that boy from Napier, she'd taken a big risk in tackling Cyril Upjohn head-on at a recent Rotary lunch. It indicated either a high measure of self-confidence or a total and refreshing lack of political nous.

'No, I'll go myself.'

'I want a human interest slant, Norm. Two pretty faces for the front page. Bitter rivals turned team-mates, that sort of thing. Whistle up a photographer. You can do a think-piece on the overall team when you get back. They may want a sub-leader too.'

Do it yourself, you're the Sports Editor, thought Norm, although pleased to have the honour of pronouncing the paper's official line on the Olympic team, as he'd done regularly for the last twenty years. You're a lazy sod, he thought, looking down at this man in braces, with the gift of the gab and sharp line in suits, brought in seven years ago from a provincial paper to sit in the chair that he, Norm Thompson, might reasonably have expected.

Still, Sports Editors get chained to desks in noisy, neon-lit and badly-ventilated news-rooms, while he at least would spend this afternoon in the far more wholesome company of two young women with the world at their feet.

He rang to make a time to see Maggie Benton — 'No, she's not going training today,' said her so-couth mother. 'She's having a day off to celebrate with her father and I.' Me, thought Norm, a stickler for grammar despite his sloppy appearance. 'I'd like to get a picture of both the girls together, in togs, at the pool,' he said, and there was a long silence while a conference took place behind the muffled phone. Her voice, when it informed him that Maggie would be available at two-thirty at the pool, was polite but remote, as to a tradesman. 'She couldn't speak for Alex,' she said; 'Maggie had tried to ring, but her phone was permanently engaged.' No love lost there, he thought, a bundle of jealousy, a 'swimming mum' of the first water. He'd met plenty, in all sports. The male versions who hung around rugby fields were — if it was possible — the worst. He'd have to take a chance on driving out to Epsom and finding Alex at home and prepared to go to the pool for a picture.

He prised a photographer out of his dark room, and a battered staff Morris Minor, smelling of cigarettes and grubby raincoats, out of the carpark underneath the newspaper's central city office. The weather was unusually miserable for the end of May, raining and so dark he had to put on side lights to negotiate the traffic. Along the Archers' street, lined with plane trees, stood rows of fifty-year-old kauri villas and thirty-year-old California bungalows; comfortably bourgeois. Outside one of the shabbier villas, he drew up and left the photographer loading up his Rolleiflex while he went into the house.

The rain beat on the windscreen and time passed, longer than the photographer thought necessary to jack up the girl for a quick pic'. She was talking to her coach in Aussie, said Norm when he finally came back to the car. Good story — some drama, it seemed. Bill Jack's old mother finally did the decent thing and died yesterday, so he'd be back home after the funeral. Alex had been without her coach for the past six weeks, poor kid.

What about the picture, said the sleepy photographer, interested only in what he saw in his viewfinder. Took some persuading, said Norm, taking his time rolling a cigarette between brown fingers. Why, for God's sake? Just a kid, going to the Olympics, a mugshot's all we want, said the photographer.

Norm grunted. Highly strung, intense sort of kid. Been crying. Strange; the mother was a very pleasant sort of woman, large-boned, soft-voiced, no pretensions, three other kids eating lunch, school holidays; a tiny old crone hovering round, chooks out the back, gumboots in the hall, smell of baking, your average Kiwi family. Father does something in the Post Office, served in the Navy.

Rivetting, said the photographer sardonically. Norm started up the car. The mother will drive her to the pool at two-thirty, he said. The real story on Alex Archer he kept to himself. After the phone call from her coach, she'd pulled herself together with the poise of an old trooper. Yes, of course she was delighted to have made the team, along with Maggie.

He'd asked her feelings about the selections, those who'd missed out, the butterfly junior for instance. Yes, he deserved to go, she thought. How did she feel about other methods of selection, such as official target times or the one-off sudden death trials they held in America? Well, by being deliberately vague, that's how the selectors kept their power, she said quite blithely; they made up the rules as they went along and told the actual swimmers as little as possible. It was cuttingly, ironically true; also unprintable. Norm was not about to jeopardize any young athlete's career for the sake of a good quote. Across the Tasman, Dawn Fraser had been waging a very public running battle with officials for years, but she was a grown woman of twenty-two.

'I'm sure,' she went on, 'Mr Upjohn will be delighted Maggie and I have earned him a free trip to Rome.'

'That's off the record, of course, Alex,' he said gently, and he had been surprised by the challenging glint in her eyes. Fifteen or not, she knew exactly what she was saying.

What about their chances in Rome, she and Maggie? Dawn Fraser will win again, with Americans breathing down her neck. I'd like to make the final, she said. I think I can, on times, if I'm left alone to get on with the job. I can't speak for Maggie, though she's had a few chances I haven't, swimming in Australia. Not for the first time, Norm Thompson found himself intrigued by the cynical smile, remembering heaven knows what scandals as she gazed unflinchingly at him. Apart from what he'd heard from Grant Davies, there'd been other rumours over the past year or so; that boy who'd died as well as that storm in a teacup at the nationals, the stand-in coach who'd thrown in the sponge because she was 'impossible' to work with, and her public pronouncements about the All Black team to South Africa. Unwise, but no doubt shrewdly calculated. In ten, even five years' time, she'll be a hell of a woman, he thought.

---

After the announcement I was out cold for less than a minute. When I came to, it was to find Gran waving eau-de-cologne under my nose and the telephone receiver by my ear. Dad, who'd listened on his transistor at work, was on the other end. It seemed Mum had already filled him in about my eavesdropping problems with Mr Upjohn. Being Dad, he didn't waste time with a whole lot of 'if onlys'. 'You've done it, Alex.'

'We've done it.' I just felt exhausted.

My first phone call was to Sydney, but even while finding the number I had to take five long calls one after another and allow myself to be hugged by the kids who came rushing in from the garden, and neighbours who knocked on the front door. After the Sydney call, which gave me the equally good news that Mr Jack would be home in a few days, there was that reporter Norm Thompson at the door, jacking up a picture at the pool, and then the phone again, endlessly.

What demon made me keep Mum waiting out in the car for three or four minutes? Was it just vanity, carefully rubbing in some Max Factor erase stuff to get rid of the shadows under my eyes? I'd been using it quite often these days, even at school where make-up is *verboten*, because I couldn't bear the sight of myself in the mirror, all hollows and bloodshot eyeballs, like a European refugee.

Or was it some devil which made me engineer a grand entrance, keep all of them waiting? Anyway, it was two-twenty-five by the time I escaped from the telephone by leaving it off the hook, and two-forty by the time we arrived at the pool. Mum, who hates being late, was annoyed.

'You'll have to apologize to Mr Thompson and the photographer,' she said stiffly. 'I'll go and park the car.' Frankly, I was more interested in finding Maggie, since we had a lot to celebrate. I ran through the rain into the pool, and straight past the waiting group. Maggie was in her track suit. It was, surely the most natural thing in the world to want to hug and share our achievement. We'd both done it, together, and in our separate ways. So we hugged. The photographer took a picture. 'You won't use that,' I said, laughing.

'I hope not,' said Mrs Benton. 'You're late, Alex.'

'Sorry,' I said. 'The phone kept ringing, honestly.'

'Alex, this is our photographer, Graham Wills,' said Norm Thompson, who had come to the house earlier and quizzed me about a few things like selection processes. I don't think I was all that tactful.

'Hi,' I said, holding out my hand. Today I was giving a good imitation of a 15-year-old girl bubbling with excitement, partly because that's what they all expected and partly because I didn't like Mrs Benton's opening shots, and I needed time to find out why. 'Maggie, wasn't it awful, waiting while they read out all those other people, the fencers and rowers and everybody. I thought I would die.'

'I can't believe it. I didn't expect to get in.'

'Of course you did,' said Mrs Benton quickly.

'I'm glad ... Rome, here we come,' I said. 'Rome! The other side of the world!'

'Can you get changed quickly, Alex?' said Mrs Benton. 'Our friend doesn't have much time, and neither do we.'

'Why, where are we going?' asked Maggie. Clearly it was news to her.

'We're meeting your father in town, and some business associates.'

'Sure,' I said, and left to get changed, puzzled at the change in her tone. She'd been rather friendlier of late. What she hadn't said today was anything like well done, Alex, congratulations, after all these years it's great you've both made it. Strange.

Even stranger, when I rejoined the group, was Maggie having some solo shots taken in her togs only, being asked to bend her knee a little more, tilt her chin up, weight on the right hip, no the right, smile now. Pretty, and posed, like a *Seventeen* model, and Maggie really embarrassed, I could tell. I couldn't understand why her mother allowed it, but the look on her face said she approved.

'OK, now together,' said the photographer. 'Alex, you're the taller, what about sitting on the railing, Maggie can stand in front.' He took a few steps back, remembered just in time he was on the brink of the pool, and positioned himself squatting on his haunches, peering down into his viewfinder. 'Great, good, what about an arm around your girlfriend, Alex?'

'No,' I said. He looked up. I shook my head. He didn't need to know that exactly a year ago the rumours had started: that being tall and broad shouldered and always hugging my girlfriends and playing male parts in school plays — I was a bit short on feminine hormones.

After a slight pause, he thought better of pushing me any further.

'Well, let's see. Just incline your heads a little towards each other. That's it, more. More. More. Two brilliant smiles, you're off to Rome.' I must still have been looking steely.

'Alex? Big smile. Bend that knee a little more.'

'No,' I said again. 'I'm a swimmer, not a beauty queen, which is patently obvious in these togs.'

He looked up at Mr Thompson. 'What's the matter with this girl?'

'You can take me as I am,' I said. 'I'm not Marilyn Monroe, and I don't intend to look silly trying.'

'You're being very childish,' said Mrs Benton.

To my relief, Norm Thompson took over.

'Looks fine to me, Graham. We'll probably only use head and shoulders anyway.'

'Good,' I said. Graham took a few more, without saying anything except 'Ready, here we go'. His bald head was shining with anger.

'Look,' I said, 'If we were 15-year-old male swimmers, you wouldn't be asking us to flex our biceps and look manly like Mr Atlas. You'd just take us as we are. That's all I'm asking, the same treatment.'

'Neurotic,' I heard him mumble under his breath as he began to put his equipment away in his bag.

'That's great, that'll be fine,' said Norm Thompson. 'Quite right, Alex, we don't want our Olympic athletes reduced to cheesecake, do we?'

'He gave it a good try,' I said, earning a look of darkest fury from the photographer. I don't suppose he was used to young females refusing to be pushed around into the approved moulds.

'I think we should go, Maggie,' said Mrs Benton. She'd had enough of me too. 'Oh, Mrs Archer, I didn't see you there.'

'Well, hullo, this is a big event, a big day. Maggie, well done, dear,' said Mum, hugging her. 'I'm very pleased you've both made it. Mrs Benton, congratulations to you too.'

'Excuse me, ladies. We're off,' said Mr Thompson. The photographer had already gone, without a backward glance. 'We've got others to see, some of the athletes. Thanks for your time. I'm sure the picture will be quite OK.' We all said polite goodbyes.

'Yes, we're very happy,' said Mrs Benton, turning to Mum, lying through her teeth. 'Now Harold and I can make our own travel plans. We were intending to go to Europe anyway, but of course, this is the best possible reason.'

'How wonderful,' said Mum. 'Someone to cheer for you, girls.'

'Maggie will be staying with us in Rome. We have some old

Singapore friends there, diplomats.'

'But . . . I'll be with the team in the Olympic village, with Alex.'

'I don't think so. You're too young.'

'Oh Mum! I want to be with the team.'

'Of course she does,' I said, lightly. 'There're five athletes going too, but they're all much older than us. I don't want . . .'

'What you want, Alex, and what Maggie's father and I think is best for her, might be two different things.'

'Mum, you can't . . .'

'We're not discussing this now. Go and get changed, please Maggie.' She'd certainly put a dampener on things. With a despairing glance at me, Maggie went slowly.

'She's just a child, not like this sophisticated young lady here,' said Mrs Benton.

'I'm only four months older than Maggie.'

Her brief silence spoke volumes. Then, 'I always enjoy your daughter, Mrs Archer.'

'I'm delighted to hear it,' said Mum, hoodwinked. 'So do we, despite her whirlwind life.'

I couldn't stand it. 'I'm going to have a swim, not training, just fun. Twenty minutes, OK Mum?'

'Can't keep her out,' said Mum, with mock resignation. I dived in and left them to it.

---

The photographer got his own back, in the end. The next morning I went training with Dad, and came back to the breakfast table to find Maggie and me on the front page. It was the one taken when I'd first rushed into the pool. I looked like a gorilla, enclosing Maggie in my great shoulders, teeth bared in a hideous grin. WATER BABIES CELEBRATE, said the heading. Some baby!

Dad and Mum tried to make light of it, as they'd done in the past when less then flattering things about me had appeared in the papers. 'They say there's no such thing as bad publicity.'

'What do I want publicity for?' I said.

'Didn't you realize the photographer was there?' said Mum pointedly.

'What am I supposed to do, creep around the place because some photographer might be lurking! Take it away!'

'Water baby,' sang my darling little brother over his porridge. 'I love you too,' I snarled and took my porridge into my bedroom.

Luckily I didn't have to face the masses at school for another week and by then it would be old news. But the phone calls, telegrams, interviews and visits continued for several days. I didn't want to see Keith at all, but he came anyway. He reminded me of all the things about last December, especially what he'd told me recently about the driver of the Jaguar, that I was trying to forget. We sat awkwardly around the kitchen table for ten minutes or so, then he got the message that I wasn't going to suggest we went somewhere where there weren't children, Mum and Gran coming and going, the radio going, a meal being prepared. He gave me up as a bad job and left.

Julia, however, could be useful, and I rather hoped she might bury the hatchet and turn up. We'd hardly spoken for months and I knew that she had sentenced herself to heavy swotting during the holidays, towards those brilliant science marks she had to achieve in November. I heard Mum say, 'Go on through, Julia,' and she appeared, uncertain, in the doorway.

'Great stuff, Alex. I'm really, really pleased.'

'Thanks.'

'That was a lousy picture in the paper yesterday.'

'I thought so too. It was revenge.'

She laughed. 'Who have you been upsetting this time?'

'Everybody. I'm past caring.' Help, I felt tears coming. 'Oh, hell, Julia, why can't people leave me alone?'

'It's obvious why.'

'Oh, I wish . . . tell me. Why haven't I had a period for three months? All that Human Biology you do — can you tell me?'

She looked totally shocked. 'What!! You're not . . .'

'Don't be stupid. I haven't been anywhere near a boy since . . .' Still I can't say it, still I can't control the tears.

She put her arm around my shoulders as I wept. 'I don't know. Haven't you asked your Mum?'

'I can't talk to her any more.'

'Your Gran? No? What about your coach?'

'He's been away. His mother died.'

'When's he coming back?'

'This week some time.'

'Well, ask him. You might need a check-up. You *do* need a check-up, you're so skinny and scrawny I'm surprised your mother hasn't hauled you off already.'

'That drunken bastard, Julia, do you know he's shot through to Aussie? Killing, mudering someone, and he's going to get away with it? And his wife can't or won't say anything and doesn't have to.'

'Who are you talking about?'

'The driver of the car that . . .'

'Who told you?'

'Keith.'

'He would. The creep. The tactless, thoughtless, stupid little creep.'

'Did you know too?'

'Oh yes, I've known for months.' She waited for my tears to abate, which of course they did. 'I'm sorry, Alex, it's rotten. Oh, yes.' Changing the subject. 'My mum was at Mrs Benton's for coffee recently. She said the house is amazing.'

'Yeah, it is,' I said gloomily.

'She said Mrs Benton's a bit odd. She kept talking about you all the time.'

'All lies, I bet.'

'No, all compliments. Couldn't say a thing against you. Wanted to know more, since you and Maggie are going to Rome together.'

Mrs Benton knew all about me already. I didn't like the sound of this.

———

The house is full of things Italian. Mum has organized the kids into getting huge posters which line the hall, my bedroom, the kitchen — crude wobbly images of the dome of St Peters, the Colosseum, famous Roman arches, the leaning tower of Pisa, the canals of Venice and the great bronze Bapistery gates of Florence. She gets books from the library in heaps — every travel book that's ever been written — and brochures from travel agents, and reads them over meals. Dad has hauled out his diaries from his time in the Mediterranean during the war — his ship was based in Malta, he says, but he did visit Naples and some of the southern ports and went to an opera house, though he can't remember what he saw.

The music! The music teacher at school and Mum both get records of Callas and Tebaldi and Giuseppe di Stefano and the house rings with arias from *Butterfly, Tosca, Aida, Rigoletto, Traviata* until the neighbours complain and the kids go and play with their friends. Mum finds out that during the Games they are doing a massive production of *Aida,* outdoors, and so she gets a complete recording and for several nights we all sit down — not the kids — and listen to the whole thing, following the story and the words on a booklet that comes in the box. By the end I'm a jelly.

And the artworks! Mum gets books on Michelangelo and Leonardo and Giotto and we pore over them together. She gets a phrase book and starts practising Italian, jollying me along with her, which dissolves the kids into helpless laughter. 'Parlo Italiano.' 'Buon giorno, signora.' 'Scusi, signore, mi può dire che ora è, per piacere.' 'Certo, signore, sono le due e venti.' Etcetera.

And the clothes! The day I was selected Gran hauled out every pattern she has for me, discards most of them, and takes me into the material shop in town to work down her list of clothes I'll need. 'It's going to be hot, so mostly drip-dry cottons, none of those jeans, my girl' she says firmly. 'Girls look like girls in Italy. We want you to look nice too, don't we.' We come home armed with about ten patterns — dresses, skirts, shorts, tops — and as many lengths of material. Where she gets the money from in one fell swoop, I don't know. How she fits in all this extra sewing for me along with her programme of baby dresses and all the other things she does, is no mystery. I often hear the sewing machine whirring away when I'm up prowling the house at midnight, unable to sleep.

I wonder at all this love and preparation and sharing in my trip — but how can I ever shout at them all, it's no use, no use, turn off the record-player, take all the books away, rip down the posters; stop it, Gran, hunched over your Singer in the middle of the night, stop it, all of you, in my bones I know I'm not going. I've been betrayed once; don't lead me on, down a road that doesn't lead to Rome.

Dad and I took Mrs Jack out to the airport to meet Mr Jack, because she's one of those wives who doesn't drive. She was looking plumper than ever, hair specially done, but anxious. She was, she said, 'one of those people who eats'. The past weeks had seemed an eternity.

'Me too,' I said.

'I don't like the nights much. It's the first time I've been alone at nights.'

'Pity you couldn't have gone over too,' said Dad.

'Well, the fares aren't cheap, and someone had to look after the cats. Besides, I don't really . . . his family . . .' I thought, it's what people *don't* say that's interesting.

'The aircraft landed half an hour ago,' said the clerk at the TEAL desk. 'It was early, strong tail winds.' I looked around the airport lounge, a pretty bleak and cheerless place despite the people waiting for passengers. Three months and I'll be out here, going! I can say it now, going to Rome! Are you excited, Alex? If not, why not?

Mr Jack was one of the last out of Customs. He looked tired and thinner. We hung back, but over Mrs Jack's shoulder I saw him looking at me. He was never much good at hiding his thoughts, and what I saw was a frown of concern and disbelief, before a weary smile.

'Alex, champ, you made it,' he said, tears in his eyes, and mine too, as we had a good cuddle. 'Jim, good to see you,' he said shaking Dad's hand. He looked back at me, up and down, like a trainer might look at a racehorse.

'You've lost weight,' he said.

'So've you,' I said lightly. 'I'm sorry about your Mum.'

'It's been pretty rugged. Even if she'd had a good innings. Well, Alex, tomorrow morning? Down to work?'

'I haven't exactly been sitting around . . .'

'I can see that,' he said quickly. 'But it's different now. And better, we know where we're going. You've done a great job, Jim, and no doubt Steve too.'

'Ahhhh — well . . .' I said.

He looked up from checking his bags. 'Didn't work out?' I shook my head. 'Interesting,' he said, glancing sideways at Dad. 'We've some fences to mend, eh?'

It was more than that. Mr Jack was there on the side of the pool the next morning, at six, sure enough, and no one was gladder than me to see him there. But he told Dad he was shocked to the core by my gaunt appearance and hollow bloodshot eyes. And my surly manner hadn't improved, if anything, it was worse. He should have known that I'd rub Steve up the wrong way, and vice versa.

Worse, my stroke had gone to the dogs and he was amazed how I'd managed to produce the times I did in those final time trials, if *that* was how I was getting through the water. Finally, when did I have my last period; *four* months ago? Hardly surprising given stress and me being a stone less than my normal racing weight, and I still seemed, no don't say anything Alex, I just want you to listen; I think, Jim, the child is still pining, still grieving, and might need some professional help if she can't begin to cope with it soon. Anyway, I'm to have a complete medical check-up. This week.

All this was the night after he got home, another of those 'putting cards on the table' sessions. 'I'm not pulling any punches, Alex,' he said. 'You can hear everything I have to say to your father. It's too late for pussyfooting around.'

He looks about as tired and grey and old as I feel.

'I gather the team leaves for Rome on the tenth of August, which gives us just under three months. We'll cut back to once a day training, and make the other session weights and calisthenics. Just for two or three weeks, give her eyes a rest too. I don't suppose she's doing any stupid things we don't know about, like playing hockey?'

'Not that I'm aware.'

'Well, check up. Alex, please sit down.'

'Have I disappeared? Can't you see me sitting in this chair?'

'Oh, yes I can, and I remember about ten months ago sitting in the same chair looking at you with a broken leg, up to your thigh in plaster. Remember? And how did it get broken?'

Hockey, because I wasn't prepared to give it up.

'And did any of us know what was going on?' He turned back to Dad. 'Talk to her school if necessary. She needs no extra pressures there. She needs to eat more, and sleep more. I'll increase her vitamins.'

'I'm not playing hockey, or any other damn thing besides swimming,' I mumbled.

'You're going to Rome, Alex,' he said, unperturbed. 'Worth it? Is life worth living?'

I couldn't reply, because I didn't really know the answer.

'You've got to decide. And soon.'

---

I make one decision the next day.

'I'm not going.'

'Alex, please.'

'If that silly cousin of mine goes and gets herself pregnant, why should we have to drive all the way to Hamilton for her wedding?'

'You don't know she's pregnant.'

'Oh, Mum. An invitation arrives dripping with gold for a wedding in two weeks' time. I saw the look you gave Gran. And Auntie Pat rang the other night, late, to break the glad tidings.'

'How did..?'

'I heard Dad talking to her.' Does she assume that I *sleep* at nights? I'm sorry Pat, he said, very sorry, of course we'll come, you're having *how* many people? In the *cathedral*?

Mum's lips are twitching, despite herself.

'You're coming,' she says, pleasantly.

'I'm not. Wild horses ...'

'Alex, on this occasion you're not being given the choice. The family is going, you're family, and that's that.'

I go into my bedroom, slam the door and literally pound the walls. I'm not ready for any wedding, shotgun or not, Hamilton or wherever, in a cathedral or a tent, in false white or brazen scarlet, with a baby or without a baby, with two guests or two hundred. Then I march out to see Gran in her little baby dress factory.

'Why is it so important, Gran? *Why?*'

Her tiny feet are pumping the sewing machine treadle, flat out. Against the windows on three sides of her bedroom, added on specially when she came to live with us, the rain beats, the bare peach tree branches clack.

'God, it's cold in here,' I say. No wonder she is wearing two jumpers and a great thick long cardigan over her skinny frame, tweed skirt, thick stockings and fluffy slippers.

'You can put the heater on.' A pitiful one-bar heater stands unused.

'Tell me *why*. No one would ever miss me.'

'Well. Your cousin's having a baby. Her parents are making the best of it, as yours would for you. No listen, Alex. Families close ranks at times like these. They honour the customs, they put on a brave face.'

'But we're not her family. Mum doesn't even like Auntie Pat.'

'Your father is her brother. That's family.'

'And we tag along.'

Gran nods, roaring up another yellow organza seam, down a pink one, up a blue one, pumping at the treadle like an ancient harmonium, expertly clipping the seams and threads away, while I sit on.

'It's ... I don't want ...'

The rhythm of the needle never falters. 'You fear the young couple might clearly be in love. You fear something worse, they might not be, it's an empty ritual. And you are dreading all those fawning, well-dressed strangers, "Virginia's clever cousin, I've read about you in the papers".'

She often surprises me, Gran.

'Yes?' She looks at me sideways over the top of her sewing glasses.

'They'll never miss me.'

'Your Mum 'n' Dad will.'

'I didn't think they cared, that much.'

She lets that one lie in the air between us. Nothing is said, but I feel deeply reproached, not harshly but sadly. Even you, Gran, I've finally got offside even with you.

I'm still not going.

I make another decision, first day back at school, when the combined smiles and whispers and pointed fingers and congratulations of too many staff and too many Third Formers become altogether too much.

'I'd like to try,' I tell Miss Macrae after assembly and all that *that* entailed.

'Good, splendid. I presume your parents are happy? You've discussed it with them?'

It's easier to nod. I'm sure they would be if I explained it to them; that it was only three scenes from a very worthwhile play and all I have to do before I go away is learn a few lines and go to a rehearsal once a week; and although you can see my permanent pink eyeballs, what you can't see is my brain getting pickled in salt water; of course they're happy.

It's only the first scene, where Joan first appears as a simple country girl and talks her way into an audience with the Dauphin; the short scene by the river, Joan as the soldier, waiting impatiently for the wind to change to begin the battle; and the Trial Scene, Joan as prisoner, defeated in battle and on trial for her life. Not the whole play, three shortish scenes.

There's another reason, too, why it's become important to me. After the May holidays, all that most people can talk about is the dances they went to, how many and where, who with, who other people went with and how often, and what they wore. People don't expect me to join in; they know I'm right out of the social whirl, that I wasn't invited to one single dance; they know I had a boyfriend, once; now they seem to know something else about me.

It's lunch break, inside because the rain is belting down, the macrocarpa trees around the playing fields are bending to the gale, the netball courts are under water and the hockey field is awash. Though it's against the rules, I've gone back into the classroom to read, to get away from the hen talk in the hall.

Julia sits herself down beside me. I know it's Julia because no one else bellows and wheezes like that.

'What you reading? Oh, *Saint Joan*.'

'Mmm.'

'I hear Miss Macrae wants to do some of it in her Shaw thing.' I grunt. 'Has she chosen people?'

'Mmmm.'

'Are you doing Joan?'

'Maybe.'

She's not impressed, I can tell by the silence.

'So why shouldn't I do Joan?' I say suddenly looking at her straight.

'Oh, no reason, if..'

'If what?'

She's horribly, embarrassingly embarrassed. What is she trying to tell me as she struggles for air?

'There's rumours.'

'There's always rumours.'

'Joan will make it ... worse.'

I understand. Type-casting, if you're ignorant enough to think there was something queer about Joan. So, rumours about my lack of femininity have surfaced again. Last year only Andy and Julia knew that I knew what was being said; only Andy ever dared raise the subject. Please, *not* again.

'Joan is not ... for heaven's sake, the first paragraph of the Preface, look here.' I wave a shaking book at her, oh, how the leaves of the little book are shaking. 'See, "the pioneer of rational dressing for women ... she refused to accept the specific ..."' I stumble twice over specific. Julia waits.

'And who from, this time?'

She is wheezing, pumping, fumbling with her pill bottle.

'My mother ...'

'Your *mother*? Oh, I see, she's upset and worried that one of her daughter's friends might be ... and warning you to stay away, that it?'

Don't make it any easier for her, will you?

'No, no. It's just, she heard ...'

'At another of those precious coffee mornings? Or little groups tittley-tattling over bridge?'

The bell starts ringing and some people open the door into the classroom. 'You're interrupting! Get out!' They have as much right to be in the classroom as I have, but they flee at least temporarily. I'm leaning over Julia's shoulder like a baddie threatening a goodie in a cheap Hollywood movie. 'Was it at Mrs Benton's?'

'No, I told you, she's all sweetness and light.'

That's what worries me. Don't relax yet. With head tipped back, Julia is trying to gather enough saliva in her mouth to swallow down the pill. If I had an ounce of human kindness in me I'd offer to get her a drink of water from the cloakroom.

She swallows, coughs and says hoarsely, 'Someone whose daughter goes to Maggie's school, Mum wouldn't say.'

'Naturally. Of course she wouldn't.'

I go back to *Joan*. My rigid fingers are still holding open the first page of the Preface ... *and innumerable obscure heroines who have disguised themselves as soldiers and sailors, she refused to accept the specific woman's lot, and dressed and fought and lived as men did.*

'Why did you tell me, Julia? What am I expected to do about it? Grow my hair. Get a boyfriend. Start wearing lipstick all the time. Throw a brick at all the Third Formers who follow me around. Prove something.'

'I thought you should ...'

'No.' Know, no, NO.'

'No one else'll tell you,' she bursts out, defending herself.

'So you've told me. You've *told* me. *Now what?*' I toss *Joan* inside my desk, slam down the lid, fling wide the door, push through the people waiting outside the door, ignore the booming voice of Miss Macrae following me down the corridor and take myself for another very long bike ride in the rain, skip calisthenics, fool Mum that I'm getting 'flu and end up cold, shivering, sleepless, tearless, sexless, friendless, hopeless, helpless, curled up rocking like a baby on the floor behind the locked door of my bedroom.

A skeleton called Alex gets up in the morning, goes to training, goes to school, hears nothing, says nothing, learns nothing, does nothing. Another cardboard person called Alex goes through the motions of appearing normal-if-a-bit-withdrawn; something tells her that she must.

The night before the wedding she tries to throw a sickie. Her sinus has been playing up genuinely, her eyes look as though she has some terrible medieval disease, and the idea of her poor pregnant cousin being hauled to the altar in white satin and lace sickens her. It'll be one of those weddings that ends up in Gran's *Weekly News*, BELLS RING FOR JUNE BRIDES.

'We'll leave after your training, about nine thirty,' says Mum. 'Pat's putting on a light lunch at the house beforehand.'

She's picking at her dinner, not hungry anyway.

'Eat up, Alex,' pleads Gran. 'Spinach makes your hair curl.' The idea of her with curls is so ludicrous she doesn't even bother to snort. 'Please, dearest.'

'There's 'flu around at school.'

Mum says nothing, but after dinner she arrives in her bedroom shaking down a thermometer. She had intended to cook the thermometer under the hot tap to read a hundred and two; Mum beats her to it. Her temperature is normal. Mum assesses her professionally. She knows that look.

'What are you going to wear tomorrow?'

'I'm not feeling well.'

'You're not looking well, but that's a separate issue. I'm asking you to come tomorrow, for your father's sake.'

'I've got nothing to wear to a wedding.'

'This do?' Mum goes out into the hallway and brings back a dress on a hanger, a simple pinafore in a soft plaid of blues and greens. Her fingers tell her it's fine wool, probably expensive. 'Should be warm enough, with a plain blouse underneath, your black court shoes.'

'Gran-made?'

Mum nods, her trump card. Cardboard Alex sighs, vanquished. It's a Simplicity pattern Gran has used for her before; she chose the material well, and probably spent her last pound on it. That's what she's been doing this past week, sewing a wedding pinafore on top of all those baby dresses and clothes for Rome. She had thought Gran was upset with her.

'I'm not wearing a hat.'

'I'm not asking you to.'

---

The voice on the telephone, thought Joyce Benton, belonged to someone who was flustered, who didn't understand the subtleties of negotiation, keeping doors open, gentle persuasion.

'She was very off-hand,' said Jane Sutherland.

'Yes, she can be, but what was the outcome?'

'Not exactly 'no', but well, indifferent. Rather rude, really. Unwilling to commit herself to a function so far ahead.'

'Six weeks?' Joyce Benton stared at the Chinese painting which hung above the telephone table in her hallway, her mind working hard on the implications of this setback. 'Well, it was a grand idea of yours, Jane.'

'Of course, we can still get the swim-suits and just Maggie will be fine, with one or two of the other girls. I'm sure we can find a suitable girl.' They may be prettier, she thought, but none of them have Alex's figure, her height and slenderness, her background of ballet; not to mention the coup of two Olympic girls. She'd been taken back by the girl's sullen voice, no life in it at all.

'You don't want me,' she had said flatly. 'I'm not the model type. You want ... you know, girls with waists and pretty smiles and curls.'

'Perhaps,' Joyce Benton was saying in her clipped remote way, '... what date have you set, Jane?'

'Last week in July. The 29th. A Friday afternoon.'

Cutting it fine, thought Joyce Benton. 'Maggie and I will be back from Queensland on the 24th.'

'You're going to Australia?'

'Tomorrow, you're lucky to have caught me. Maggie can't train another day in that pool. The specialist says she runs the risk of permanent damage.'

'Dear me, what to?'

'Her eyes. Every session is sheer torture. It's salt water, badly chlorinated and then heated. And they don't get any special privileges, the public jump in, get in the way.'

'It sounds appalling.'

'After two laps, Maggie can't even see. By the time she's done two and half miles, her eyes look quite dreadful. So we're going back to Queensland, the same pool and a rather special coach, where I took her last year.'

'Lucky girl,' said Jane Sutherland. 'I suppose Alex just has to ...'

Joyce Benton cut in sharply. It had crossed her mind that she could have offered to take Alex to Australia with Maggie; her family couldn't afford it; her conscience was clear. 'Jane, ring me when we get back. I really don't want to commit Maggie either. The team leaves for Rome on August the tenth, not a great deal of time, obviously.'

'Just one rehearsal, Joyce, and it's all in school time. Did I tell you the Head is delighted? We're sending out printed invitations and the money is going to the Crippled Children Society.'

'I'm so glad,' murmured Joyce Benton, weary. There was some way round this problem, she knew, but her immediate concern was tomorrow's departure for Brisbane. 'I think you're doing a wonderful job, Jane. Please excuse me, I have to go and pick up Maggie.'

Home after training, I find the house unnaturally quiet, with the three others farmed out for the day, and both Gran and Mum looking unnaturally smart. Gran has hauled out her 19-year-old brown tweed best suit, and a strange little hat, and Mum has an eight-year-old navy suit and (as they say in the *Weekly News*) 'white accessories'. There'd been some discussion as to whether Dad should hire 'morning dress', whatever that meant, but in the end he climbs into his one grey suit. I envy him his lack of fuss; the only frivolous decision he has to make is his tie.

Dressed up, we pass with a push. My pinafore hangs in interesting folds over hips that have never been slimmer. Mum produces some nice stockings and lends me black gloves and handbag to go with my black court shoes; I cut off a few spiky bits of hair and it looks worse than ever. Mum has also got Gran a spray of pink carnations to pin on her lapel, and a single white carnation for Dad as the bride's uncle. I sleep all the way to Hamilton, my head on Gran's bony, tweedy shoulder, smelling of Yardley's lavender water.

I haven't seen Auntie Pat's house in years. Not much of it is visible today, because a huge tent-like thing, decorated with golden ribbons and hanging baskets of yellow and white flowers, has been put up in the garden. 'They took a risk, in June. Lucky with the weather,' says Dad, as we walk up the driveway carefully lined with neat plants. The sunshine here is crisper, colder than home. Inside the house, which is boring brick and tile, the first thing I notice is a busy, bilious green, floral carpet arguing with all the wallpapers. The 'light lunch' for relatives from out of town consists of four tables groaning with sausage rolls, club sandwiches, sponge cakes, butterfly cakes, the *Edmonds Cook Book* come to life. She must have been cooking for weeks.

Cousin Virginia, plain to start with, looks as brittle as a celluloid bride doll. In guipure lace, satin, net and seed pearls, diamante tiara, the works; she's agreed to be a triumph. The dress has a twenty inch waistline and a Merry Widow girdle underneath, no concessions to a baby there. Her beehive hair-do, even from across the room, is stiff with beads of hairspray; make-up is a demure pink mask. I find myself staring at this Christmas tree fairy, wondering how she'd arrived at this point: the groping in a car, two weeks overdue, three, four; the telling scenes, him, both sets of parents; the tears over the alternatives of having the baby in disgrace and adoption, or a fast wedding before it shows; who had won, in the end? So there she stands. The Bride, on the happiest day of her life, pinned against the venetian blinds while the photographer sets up his gear. She sees me staring. I deserve a poked-out tongue, what I get is a terrible blank gaze in return. She makes my blood run cold.

Auntie Pat, in cream silk, is beside herself. The bouquets haven't arrived.

'Oh, here's Alex, *dear*, Helena, Jim, lovely to see you, thank you, all that way. We're all a bit, oh dear. One of the bridesmaids keeps feeling faint, one of *those* days. Oh, darling, you got in the team, well done, lovely to see you, Ginnie's *so* glad ...'

Ginnie's not with us at all, I think. Her bridesmaids, three of them, crowd the lounge, bulging in golden satin like ripe apricots, amid the stench of hairspray. Like Ginnie, they are not all that much older than me, and too carried away to take much notice of me in my plaid pinafore. I'd once thought that when I married it would have been in Grecian style like one of those old statues in the Museum. Plain white silk, straight and simple, not a flounce nor a shred of lace anywhere, flowers in my long hair, no jewellery, no veil; a man in white, with brass buttons, a naval sword. A garden wedding, under the pohutukawa and magnolia trees ... A wicked echo of Julia's last words makes me pluck a white flower from the garden on the way to the church and poke it behind my ear. 'That's nice, dear,' says Gran, not understanding. 'Pretty.'

Somehow we all get to the cathedral, which is the biggest church

I've ever been in, full of flowers and people in silk suits and swathed turbans and furs and what I now know is called morning dress or penguin suit. Grey top hats, like the Ascot scene in *My Fair Lady*, and everywhere the smell of perfume and face powder and mothballs. There is a huge choir in red gowns, and a small thin person who turns out to be the groom, Ginnie's ballroom dancing partner, naughty man, who looks equally terrified.

We have to sit up the front, among 'family' on 'the bride's side'. The first thing that happens is that Virginia is forty-five minutes late. *Forty-five*. The organ plays, the choir sings, and sings again, a vicar makes two reassuring announcements and the guests, relishing the prospect of a complication, start to talk softly and turn around to see if anything's happening. Finally, Auntie Pat scuttles alone up the side aisle and collapses on the pew in front of us; hat feathers, fur stole, silk sleeves all a-quiver; what *has* been going on?

The organ pounds out the wedding march and we all leap to our feet and sing madly — Praise my Soul, the King of Heaven — before the bridge changes her mind completely or the groom gets fed up. I turn and look: behind several robed vicars walks a puce-faced Uncle Arnold with a veiled livin' doll leaning slightly on his arm, followed by the apricots, looking less than ecstatic. The service proceeds, formal and hushed and relentless, up and down for hymns, prayers, readings. Auntie Pat's glistening fur stole betrays her. 'With this ring, I thee wed ...' Although we are only a few feet from Ginnie and her husband of a few seconds, we can barely hear her responses, while her mother weeps.

When the bridal couple walk down the aisle at the end, Ginnie is leaning slightly inwards in much the same way as she leaned on her father, smiling brilliantly as though her face had cracked. His face, little fox-trotting Mervyn, is darkly flushed. I feel very sorry for him, until I discover that 'family' are expected to follow the bridal party, solemnly in pairs. I cannot escape having to file out after Mum and Dad, arm in arm with tiny Gran, which must look hilarious. I snap my sunglasses on my head to cover eyes which are both sore and wet with tears of anger, and somehow we make it down the nineteen miles of rich ruby carpet, through a forest of curious eyes. Flowers in the hair are not a usual substitute for a hat, except on a young girl; I'm too tall for a girl but not a woman either.

Outside the cathedral and again back at the marquee begins the waiting: for family portraits; for the bridal party to go for formal studio pictures and come back an hour later; for the receiving lines. Meanwhile there are the waiters bearing silver trays of shallow glasses of French champagne, greetings, introductions, gushings, eyeings up and down. I don't fit in here, we don't, we four Archers from ordinary old Epsom, Auckland; among these rich silk suits that are quickly getting spotted with food, osprey hats snagged on tent poles, English stiletto shoes pegging their wearers into the damp grass, penguin suits smeared with spilt drink, squashed top hats and little fox faces hanging down the furred backs of well-fed and dotty old women. The coat off an animal's back is bad enough, but keeping its dried-up head, whiskers, eyeballs and all, is *disgusting*.

I stick close to Gran, but she is waltzed away to meet some old cronies, so there's only Mum 'n' Dad 'n' me crushed along with three hundred others into the marquee because that's where the food is, and outside a cold niggling wind is blowing away any warmth in the late afternoon sun. I overhear comments about 'bad form', which turn out to be not about racehorses, nor the haste of the wedding, but about Ginnie's lateness at the church. The reason why has not yet got about. People jostle past and say 'Oh, you must be Alex-who-swims, Virginia's cousin, going to the Olympics, how nice, dear. In August? Are you going Mrs Archer, no, well I hope the chaperon's on her toes, those naughty Italians; pinch your beautiful bottom they will, m' dear'.

I discover that a hard level stare registering no reaction works quite well; I am as tall as most men; they turn away puzzled, to more interesting topics like old Stanley's recent operation, or the price of lambs in the UK, or their wonderful flight up from Christchurch on the Viscount, the central North Island mountains sporting early snow and clear as a bell. The All Blacks have won their first few provincial matches in South Africa; whether or not the team should have gone without the Maoris is a dead duck, and Sharpeville never rates a mention. One or two men who read the sports pages say, oh yes, you and that Benton girl, good stuff, dear.

In the crush I get swept away from Mum 'n' Dad, towards the

billowing sides of the marquee. There is no one else my age and no other female hatless. Most of the three hundred range from middle-aged to ancient, except for a small group of Virginia's smart friends. When I can go no further, I'm up against a row of small chairs provided for the old ladies; like one myself, I sink gratefully down on the last vacant seat. The old dears next door go on nattering loudly; Ginnie always has been a bit of a problem; she was late, disgraceful really, because she decided two minutes before the bridal cars arrived that she'd rather have the baby adopted and not marry Mervyn, and poor old Arnold had to say it was a bit late for that, Virginia, with the Bishop and three hundred guests waiting at the church. Only threatening to disown her made her see sense, poor child. Dis-own? Throw out of house, write out of will? Always money, somewhere. I hate bullies. I know further why I want to do law. I find my eyes full of tears for her, and all those dumpy girls knitting bootees Julia once talked of, and myself who people consider too manly to want to have a baby, one day; Andy's baby, a boy, never to be. Fat, full tears brim over, drip down my cheeks. A youngish waitress comes over with a tray of glasses shaped like saucers. Up till now I've only had orange juice, and refused all food.

'You look as though you need one of these,' she says. 'It's not the end of the world.' She leans down and whispers in my ear. 'You'd be surprised how many weddings we do like this, two weeks' notice, bun in the oven already.' I knock back one glass and take another. 'Atta girl. Cheer up.' It's the French champagne that's been flowing like water for an hour. It's clean-tasting and fizzy; a third goes down like lemonade. It's a mistake.

'Charge your glasses, ladies and gentlemen!' So I do, because another waitress is pushing her way through the crowd, working her way along the row of flushed old ducks with a huge green bottle wrapped in a cloth. Even sitting down, I can't seem to hold my glass awfully steady. Some spills on to the grass. Perhaps someone pushed her elbow. Far away, past the solid wall of eye-level bottoms, I hear an ancient, quavery, male voice droning on. I catch about every tenth word — Virginia — our radiant bride — since a little girl. Words to that effect.

I can stand for the toast. 'The happy couple.' I have an extra one for the baby; a few people look round as though someone has said a terrible swear word, and mutter to each other. The bridegroom's speech I can't hear at all. I can still stand for the next toast, although as I do a hiccup escapes and I have a slight bout of coughing while people turn and stare. 'The bridesmaids, bless them,' and I add an extra sip for the bridegroom — poor little fox-trotting Mervyn because, with a mother-in-law like Auntie Pat, boy, is he going to need it.

I can hear the best man only too well, because he's fearsomely handsome like Gregory Peck and has an actor's voice to match. He flatters the bridesmaids to the skies and reads out some crude, tasteless telegrams, which *I* can tell don't go down too well under the circumstances, and so can the old ducks next door, who are by this time muttering and nudging each other and staring at me. The baskets of flowers and strings of coloured lights above me are now out of focus and rather small; I'm looking down the wrong end of a smudgy telescope. I am feeling both terribly ill and an urgent need to find a loo. I think I am going to be sick.

'The bride and groom will now cut the cake.'

I believe I am whirling into space; falling off my chair.

I believe I am making an effort to stay upright. Or maybe I'm trying to crawl underneath the tent flap out into the cool air. Or maybe, hearing the crack of wood beneath me, I am breaking my chair. Of course, built like a tank; she would! Or maybe I am actually vomiting French champagne on to the damp grass. I really can't remember.

I remember waking up. I'm juddering, convulsing, coming back from the dead. Someone is pushing my head down on to my knees. Voices boom in my ears.

'Stand back. Give her some air.' Male, in charge.

'What's wrong with the child?' Female, curious.

'Fainted, that's all.' Male, matter-of-fact.

'Just keeled over.' Female, startled.

'Or rather too much . . .' Female, whispering.

'Alex?' Mum, at last. 'Where have you been?'

'Ask a silly question . . .' Me, grinning.

I know it's her arm around me, her fingers taking my pulse, her voice requesting air and some help to get me outside. My head is spinning and I'm weeping quietly, as a woman's voice with a pommie accent, high-pitched like the Queen, penetrates all too clearly through the crowd noises.

'Isn't that Virginia's cousin, the Olympic girl from Auckland? Something of a madam, Joyce says. I do believe the child has been drinking.'

'Not at all,' says Mum loudly. 'This child has already swum six miles this morning.' You exaggerate, Mum! And she's not finished yet. 'She's a finely-tuned athlete, in extremely heavy training, not used to standing round for such long periods.' It's quite convincing, since I've actually been sitting for the past half hour.

'I'm training for Rome, ma'am,' I hear myself saying with great dignity, 'Maggie and I are both going to Rome. Together. Although, Maggie's in Australia and that silly prick of a selector, Mr . . .'

'That's enough, Alex!' Mum's voice, her best nurse's voice, loud and cold. Her strong arms are pulling me to my feet. She's dealt with nutcases before.

'I want to lie down,' I say, as the marquee goes round and round above my head.

'Into the house,' says Dad. They walk one on each side of me while I sing *Three Coins in the Fountain* and the guests part like the Red Sea. Behind me, I hear, 'Ladies and gentlemen, your attention please. The bride and groom will now cut the cake.' I've almost certainly spoiled Virginia's big moment and Auntie Pat's grand wedding, the youngest guest blotto on French champers.

My feet won't work properly, but we're out of the marquee, and away from those voices. The cold dusk air makes me gasp. To give her her due, Auntie Pat comes rushing out behind us.

'Helena, I'm so sorry. This is most unfortunate, shall I call an ambulance?'

'Of course not,' says Mum. 'She's just a little faint. Her period on top of seven miles of training this morning and all this standing around.' *Seven* miles now and my first period in five months! Perhaps the back of my dress is stained and I don't know it. I didn't know Mum could lie like a flatfish.

After vomiting into a flower bed on the way into the house, I slept in a spare bedroom for maybe an hour and woke around eight with a throbbing head.

'Water,' I croaked to the upright little figure of Gran keeping watch on the end of the bed. I lay there for a bit. At least the room wasn't whirling round. Mum came in, and, rather unnecessarily I thought, took my pulse again.

'How are you feeling?'

'Fantastic.'

'Virginia and Mervyn are just leaving. After that, we'll be going too.'

'I'll get up.'

'You don't have to.'

'I want to.' And I meant it, to hold my head high and have the pleasure of looking right through those smugly disapproving people. I got vertical and nearly changed my mind.

'Good girl,' said Gran. We went quietly out to the front porch where Virginia was saying tearful goodbyes under the coloured lights, and Mervyn looked as though he'd danced his last waltz. Their car, decked out with ribbons, buckets, tins, and rude signs, waited below in the driveway. Virginia was dressed in a quite revolting going-away suit of orange, with nipped-in waist, matching hat, black gloves and the highest stiletto heels I have ever seen. Female squeals went up when she threw her bouquet towards the twittering bunch of apricot bridesmaids, ripe for the picking. One had already homed in on Gregory Peck, clutching at his arm. In the shadows no one took any notice of me when tears fell; I have seen Andy again, a face among the crowds down there around the departing car. Please, leave me alone.

And that might have been the end of an awful day, except that Auntie Pat, now that she had done her duty and gone through this charade, got stuck into the gin bottle. If we'd had any sense we'd have left half an hour earlier than we did.

'Just come and sit down for ten minutes,' she pleaded to Dad. 'I've hardly seen you, Jim.' Dad hesitated. 'And Alex, are you feeling better now?'

'Yes thank you, Auntie Pat.'

'Just go into the living-room, I'll be with you in a minute. There are a lot of people leaving.' So we small talked with other relatives until she came back with a large gin in her hand and collapsed on to the sofa next to Mum.

'Thank God that's over.' We all knew what she meant. She took a large swig, lit up another cigarette, and started to talk to Mum. From my chair alongside Gran, on the other side of the floral carpet, I saw Mum's smile getting more and more inscrutable, like a camel. Then quite suddenly, unusual for someone who is big and moves rather slowly, she heaved herself out of the sofa and made a beeline for me and Gran. Auntie Pat's voice beat her to it.

'Alex,' she cried. 'Come and talk to your Auntie Pat.'

I could hardly refuse. 'We're going,' Mum muttered as we passed. 'Say your goodbyes.'

But Auntie Pat was patting the empty seat beside her, and I had to sit down. She had never taken much notice of me in the past, and I saw no reason to get all palsy-walsy now.

'So tall and handsome, our Olympic girl. I don't see enough of you, do I? I was just telling your dear mother, it was such a shame you couldn't be a bridesmaid today.'

'Why not?'

'Virginia felt, it wouldn't have looked quite right, now would it?'

What was she talking about?

'Pity you got it from both sides. Your father was a beanpole at fourteen, like our father, and then he went and married your mother, who's no thistle-down is she.'

I'm not usually thick, but I still didn't know what that had to do with me not being a bridesmaid.

'Ginnie knew you'd understand. Not being a bridesmaid.'

As if it mattered, if it meant apricot satin. 'I don't mind.'

'Such a short man she's married. He says he's five foot eight, but you'd hardly know it. Anyway, it would have been, you know, rather like David and Goliath.'

'You mean, I'm Goliath?'

'Oh, dear, no,' she giggled, meaning yes. 'But you understand. I didn't think your dear mother did, quite . . .' She took another swig of gin. 'But then I didn't expect that she would.'

One thing I've learned this past year is that sometimes saying nothing is the best way of finding out what's going on. People can't bear the sound of their own silence.

'All that swimming, made you so bulky, those shoulders ...' I think she actually shuddered.

'I like my shoulders.'

'And I hear you want to be a lawyer?'

'Yes.'

'Whatever for?'

'Use my brain. Help people in trouble. Know how to stand up to bullies. Bring murderers to justice.'

'My dear!'

'I might stand for Parliament. Earn enough money to buy a car, buy a house ...'

'A house? My dear, get a good husband, he buys the house. Like Ginnie, not so clever as you, I always knew that, but only eighteen and married already.' She didn't quite look at me as she said this. 'He mightn't look much, but his father's in furniture, the best business in town, antiques, real English quality — he's the "And Son", you know.'

Who cared? Perhaps Virginia was the smart one after all.

'Alex?' Mum's voice from across the room, sharply. 'We have to go now. Gran's rather tired.'

Auntie Pat's hand was on my knee. 'Take it from your Auntie Pat. Forget all that lawyer nonsense, dear. Men don't like girls with brains. Helena, you and Jim shouldn't encourage her ...'

'We don't, overly. Neither do we discourage her. Alex will decide for herself.'

'But how dangerous! All this sport, and then she wants to be a career girl as well, and you and Jim say nothing?'

'Pat, it's been a good day, a good wedding. You've done a magnificent job and thank you.'

'You'll regret it, when she's thirty and still on your hands.'

I said, 'When I'm thirty I'll be a lawyer and not on anyone's hands.'

'Don't let your mother down, Alexandra.'

'Let her down?'

'Mother of the bride ...'

'And you've done it superbly, Pat. Now ...'

'... that's all any mother wants, don't you, Helena?'

'What I want for Alex is something quite different and doesn't include a hasty marriage, however grand, at eighteen. Alex, go and find your father, please. Gran, we're going.'

'I do believe you're jealous of Virginia, not quite ideal circumstances, I know, but still only a year after being a deb ...'

I was rude enough to laugh.

'You can think that if you wish,' said Mum.

'I do. You were always ...'

'Pat, don't go on. You don't want to spoil your day, neither do I, any further.'

'Well, yes, Alex did steal a wee bit of the show, didn't she? One or two people have told me ...'

'One or two people have got it wrong, Pat, as they always do. Although in Virginia's case ... you are hardly in a position to start pointing a finger at my daughter. Now, where's Dad?' I'd been standing with my mouth open at this unleashing of claws, but one look at Mum's face told me to get moving. She went to get Gran, who was having her own animated last-minute goodbyes with some other old ducks.

I found Dad in the kitchen with Uncle Arnold and a group of penguins, into the whisky and beer and cigars.

'Mum wants you quick quick. We're going.'

'Now?'

'Right this minute, before she and Auntie ...' There were some curious males eyes resting on me in a way I didn't like, eager, gleeful.

'Gran's tired.'

'I'm coming.' But now Mum had followed me, and we were out of there in two minutes flat, goodbyes, thanks. As we drove off to waves and cries, I caught a last glimpse of Auntie Pat. Her hostess mask had gone, she looked exhausted, close to tears, her cream silk dress all crumpled.

Mum broke the silence. 'I went with the best of intentions, Jim. I'm sorry ... her prattle irritates me so, as it always did, and she was being inexcusably rude to Alex.'

'What about?'

'She called me Goliath. Virginia couldn't have me for a bridesmaid because I'm too tall. Men don't like girls with brains, and wanting to be a lawyer is positively weird.' But Dad found it rather funny; so, chuckling alongside, did Gran.

'She's jealous, always was, my poor sister. You're going to the

Olympics and Virginia's put them through the humiliation of a shotgun wedding. Well, it's not the end of the earth. Pat had all sorts of dreams. Ginnie was going to be another Rowena Jackson, but then she went into ballroom. She's a nice kid, but not all that bright.'

Mum said, her voice calmer. 'Give Pat her due, organizing all that in three weeks. Well, at least they didn't throw her out of the house. Some do.'

'He threatened to,' I said.

'Who did?'

'Uncle Arnold, that's why she was late, because she got cold feet and he threatened to disown her. Didn't you hear all the prattle?'

That silenced them. Then Mum sighed.

'I didn't like to ask. Poor Pat, Ginnie wed and gone, what's left?'

'A baby,' I said.

'She'll need something more than a grandchild to babysit,' said Dad, testily. 'She's only forty-six, for God's sake.'

Mum snorted. 'Well, let's see. Good works, meals on wheels. The house is immaculate and no weed dares poke up its head. She doesn't sew, doesn't knit, she's got everything money can buy, Arnold's away on business a lot and he's hardly a ball of fire. And he makes her account for every last penny of the housekeeping money.'

'Did you see all the presents?' said Gran. 'I have never *seen* such a display.'

'On the vulgar side, I thought,' said Dad, mildly. 'A bit overdone.'

We all fell silent. The oncoming lights were hurting my eyes so I snuggled up against Gran.

'You've never told us you wanted to do law, Alex,' said Mum suddenly. 'Why law?'

'Just do.'

'The power to change things, eh?' said Dad.

'Something like that,' I said sleepily.

I was drifting into sleep, feeling carsick. Tomorrow I might have a hangover.

'A finely-tuned athlete.' Mum, you did well. But something I heard in that tent is lying at the back of my memory, niggling me.

I recognized the paper immediately. The thick feel of it, the italic type, the pompous ornate letterhead, the smell of trouble.

'You'd better read it,' said Dad, as Mum shut the bedroom door behind me.

> *Dear Mr and Mrs Archer,*
> *I am writing to you in strictest confidence, with the deepest regret that such a letter is necessary. I have thought hard as to the best course of action to take about this matter. With the best interests of all our young swimmers at heart, it seemed desirable that I should write to you informally and privately to express my concern.*
>
> *We have all watched Alexandra's career develop with great interest and admiration.*

I've read that phrase before.

> *Since her nomination in March, Alexandra has displayed commendable tenacity in her quest for Olympic selection. Sadly, this has not always been matched by behaviour which is commensurate with her abilities and performance.*

'What does commensurate mean?' I asked.

'In line with, equal to,' said Mum.

'Why doesn't he say so?'

'Businessmen, academics and politicians like long words, Latin words, five words where two would have done,' said Mum.

> *I refer to her public criticism of the selectors, her outbursts on the current South African All Black Rugby tour, and her participation in the protest march last month, resulting in some unfortunate publicity. Any one of these one could possibly overlook as evidence of the high-spirited personality we know her to be. However it has come to my attention ...*

'How?' I said.

> ... *that at a recent social occasion in Hamilton she was seen to have consumed an amount of hard liquor hardly befitting a New Zealand sporting representative, particularly female, and in this state to have made further ill-considered remarks about officialdom, remarks which could be seen to be singularly lacking in gratitude to the administrators who give freely of their time and expertise to run her chosen sport.*

'I only know of one remark,' said Mum. 'Were there others?'
'No,' I said, with more confidence than I felt.

> *I am aware that her coach's absence, and the long waiting period between nomination and selection may have contributed. But now that she has, by her own admirable efforts in the pool, won her place in the team, I personally would be saddened to see her jeopardize her place by incidents out of the pool. I have to reluctantly say that should any further incidents like this occur, I shall be compelled to raise with the Olympic selectors and my fellow swimming selectors the question of her suitability to compete in Rome.*
>
> *Please understand that I write to you not in my capacity as a National Selector, but as a friend, and a parent myself, in Alexandra's best interests. Her talent is great and I know that, provided she exercises the self-control and behaviour expected of a young girl, she will be a worthy competitor in Rome. I look forward greatly to accompanying her, and Maggie, to Rome and carrying out my duties there as their manager. I hope you will accept this letter in the spirit in which it is written. I believe it would be preferable not to discuss the matter with Bill Jack; I have every confidence in your discretion and judgement as her parents to take whatever steps you feel appropriate. Neither is a reply necessary. The best reply would be that the period between now and our departure in August is free of controversy and further incident involving Alexandra.*
>
> *Yours most sincerely,*
> *Cyril Upjohn, Esq.*

Ordinary family noises went on, Robert and Jamie scrapping in their bedroom next door, the radio in the kitchen while Gran finished the dinner dishes. Mum and Dad were both looking at their feet. Eventually I broke the silence.

'Five hundred words to say, "Last warning, sweetie pie".'

'Correct,' said Mum, wearily. 'Has there been a first, Alex?'

'Who told him about the wedding?'

'Does it matter?' said Mum.

'Oh, it matters,' I said. I read the letter again. Then because Mum was smoking, I leaned over, picked up her silver lighter, and deliberately set one corner of the letter alight. We all silently watched it burn down towards my fingers. The flakey ashes fell on to my desk; I held the paper until it was burning my fingertips and I could blow the last flame away. I brushed the blackened tips of my fingers and licked them, feeling the heat on my lips.

'There,' I said. 'Mr Upjohn up in smoke.'

There was another long silence. Then Dad said,

'You shouldn't have done that, Alex.'

'He'll have a copy. He's bound to have a copy.' Then, because my normally sensible, all-knowing parents seemed to be at a loss for words, I said, 'Well, if there's nothing else, I've got homework to do.' I began to scrummage in the mess on my desk.

'Please. Alex. This can't go on.' Dad's voice, low, intense, with a catch in it.

'What can't?'

'For four months nearly, since the nationals — don't you realize you've hardly said a civil word to your family. We've had complaints from school, Miss Gillies and two of the staff, Julia has been around here expressing her concern, and that boy Keith, Mr Jack is worried sick. That letter — if the press got wind of it.'

'Why should they? It's private.'

'They will, if you continue to make scenes and ...'

'Alex Archer dropped from Olympic team, Mr Upjohn reluctantly announced today. I warned her, I sent her a letter. Young swimmer can't behave herself. Disgrace to the family name, letting the school down. Tart, show-off, loudmouth.'

'Alex!'

'Well if it's so bad, if I've been so dreadful to live with, why haven't you said something before? Do you know *why* I had two too many at that ghastly wedding ...'

'Alex, please ...'

'Because you shouldn't have made me go in the first place,

because you shouldn't have let me out of your sight, I hate crowds ... it was all a great lie, a great sham, a great act, like I am. It takes one to know one. So I had a drink or two. So I got a bit squiffy and passed out. So you had to remove me ...'

I stopped, because a cultured and penetrating English voice is ringing in my head.

'*Something of a madam, Joyce says.*'

Mrs Benton's name is Joyce.

'What's the matter, Alex? Please, please tell us.'

While I stare at her, Mum has knelt at my feet and taken my hands in hers and is desperately trying to reach me. I see her lips moving, and catch about every twentieth word: we've been trying so hard, all of us, to understand; Andy was a fine boy; but; my whole life ahead of me; asking so little; coming to terms; we've hoped, we've prayed, as every day has passed ... please, Alex, *try*.

I am trying, I scream silently. But how can you fight something so ... vicious. I can hear her now. 'Oh, Mr Upjohn, I thought you should know ...'

I haven't kept her precious daughter out of the team. So why is she still trying to destroy me?

I can't bear the sight of Mum's wet brown eyes any longer. I leave my desk, the room and the house. Mum doesn't like me walking round the streets after dark, but that night, I finally have to escape, from the suffocation of their worry, from the posters of Rome the kids have pinned up in the hallway and Gran listening to the Quiz Kids in the kitchen; from their common sense, their logic, their expectations, their impatience, coming to terms, pulling myself together, counting my blessings, and fleeing from their love; most of all, love.

---

So I run. Away, I suppose you could say. Through the rain, puddles, traffic lights, late Friday night shopping, cars, lights, people, reflections, water, rain, no idea where I'm going. Not the well-worn path to Julia's house, nor the forbidden, abandoned path to the Richmonds, nor the pool closed for the winter, nor the house For Sale, nor school. Nowhere.

Somewhere, because I'm wearing only a shirt and jumper and jeans now soaked through and getting heavier by the minute. I can think of only one person I think who might be glad to see me. I can't remember his number from that time I tried to ring him; his address will be in the phone book. Jogging now, I see a phone box in the distance. It's hard to focus on the tiny type. Jameson. Not all that far from Andy's place. A fair bike ride, a long walk.

A car pulls up alongside, a window is wound down. A wolf whistle.

'Like a lift, girlie.' I ignore him. He tries again, fifty yards on.

'Get lost.' And again, a hundred yards on, when the man in the front seat gets out and confronts me. He is shorter than me, twenty-ish, a bodgie, stovepipes, leather jacket, Elvis hair.

'I said like a lift.'

'And I said Get Lost. Go pick up a chick some place else.' He stands in my way, stretches out a hand. Even as I take a swipe at his face I'm thinking, oh, God, what now. A house to run in to? My hand is stinging, heart gi-donk gi-donk, as I run off.

'Bitch,' he yells. But I'm lucky; they don't follow — there are easier pickings in the American milk bar.

The cars thin out. House lights are still on. In a couple I see the black and white flicker of a television set against venetian blinds. I suppose it's television, I've never seen one except in a shop window; it started last month. House lights begin to go off, as sensible people go to bed, and still I walk.

Number 42 is down a right of way, small, weatherboard, no lights on. There's no car outside. I'm not so sure Keith will be that pleased to see me, but I ring the bell because I don't know what else to do. A light goes on, a shadow appears behind the glass front door. The door opens a fraction, because it's chained; suspicious eyes. I remember, his mother's separated, his father went off with a secretary.

'Yes?'

'Is Keith in?'

'No, he's — are ye not Alex, Alex Archer?'

'Yes. Can I ...'

The door has closed in my face. That's it. He's out and I'm not welcome, even here. Then I realize she's fiddling with the chain, cursing it for jamming; the door opens wide. Against the light, she's only a silhouette.

'Come in.'

'I'm soaked.'

'Nae matter. Take your sandshoes off.' It's a Scottish lilt; Keith has no Scottish accent. Have I got the right house?

'Mrs Jameson? I'm looking for ...'

'Aye. I know. Keith's out at choir practice. He's a game tomorrow, so he'll not be late.'

'*Choir* practice?'

'Aye. Well, that's what they call it, him and his engineering mates, Friday night at the pub. Hard cases.'

It's the right house. But she's pulling me in, organizing me out of my wet clothes, into the shower to warm up, into an old dressing gown — and not asking any questions. She's wearing a candlewick dressing gown herself, a couple of curlers in her hair, smells of Pond's vanishing cream, and I like her. She puts me in a frayed chair in the living-room and makes some tea; insists that I take an aspirin against a chill, and still doesn't ask me what I was doing frozen and wet and peculiar on her doorstep at ten-thirty at night. Then she says she must go to bed because she has to get up early for her Saturday job — do I want to stay the night, yes? Well I can have a blanket on the sofa, her daughter Jill is already asleep and Keith will be home soon, God and Dominion Breweries willing. She gives me a *Weekly News* to read and tucks me up with a blanket, turns out the top light and leaves. By this time I'm rather sleepy; maybe I hear the sound of a telephone clicking, a low voice, maybe I don't and care less. Maybe I hear the sound of the Morris Minor come down the drive, Keith letting himself in the back door, his mother calling him, voices. Maybe I'm aware of him standing over me for a few minutes. Maybe not. I wake with a great shudder before dawn, with no idea where I am. A small room, a different smell, frozen feet, breathing in cold damp air. Gradually it comes back: a letter, a long walk in the rain, hitting someone across the face, Keith's house, his Scottish Mum. I try to sleep again, but I have a tremble in me which won't go away. I get up, and wander through the dark house. I recognize

Mrs Jameson's room, the other bedroom must be Jill's or Keith's. The door is half open; there's enough light to see a shape in the bed. It smells like a male room; male clothes litter the floor. I sit on the end of the bed for ... ages, I don't know; strangely comforting, just waiting. Oh, this is the time I'm normally training. I chase away a little thought in my head that Mr Jack will be at the pool, waiting. And Maggie too, oh no, Maggie has gone to Australia again, hasn't she? I don't feel like training today.

Keith turns over, kicks me; prods again with his feet at this hard lump which won't go away; grunts and sits up; turns on his bedside light. We look at each other. He looks more like a half-baked gnome than ever. He's growing a beard and it's at the scraggy stage. I look around the room which is full of photographs and posters of bridges. Slender bridges, chunky bridges, the Auckland harbour bridge, Sydney, the Golden Gate. The man is obsessed with bridges. There's a guitar hanging on the wall, C.N.D. posters, books, varsity notes everywhere. Then he lies down again.

'I didn't know your mother was Scottish,' I say.

'Why should you?'

'You haven't got an accent.'

'Why should I?' Then, 'Go back to bed, Alex.'

'I don't feel like training today.'

'Don't then.' He turns over and looks at me.

'Do you want to come with me, to my footie match?'

'It's still raining.'

'So? A little bit of rain!'

'I've never been to a footie match.'

'Good. Always a first time. Part of your education. God, why did you have to wake me so early. My mouth's like an Ay-rab's armpit.'

'Too much singing.'

'What?'

'Choir practice.'

'Oh.' He grins. 'Choir practice.'

'I don't like that beard.'

'Neither do I much. Wait till it grows in red streaks.'

'Why red?'

'I'm a Scots bastard, aren't I? Mum was sort of red once.'

'What was your Dad?'

'Another bloody Scot. Go back to sleep.'

But I'm staring at a team photo on his wall. First Fifteeen 1959, fifteen fine young men, in rugby gear, boots, striped jerseys, hair cut for the occasion, combed slickly, arms folded, a rugby ball and some cups in front. In the front row is a face I knew.

Keith sees me looking at it. He sees the tears start to flood down my cheeks.

'Oh Christ,' he mumbles. He climbs out of bed, turns out the light and sits down beside me, puts his arm around me in the strong and wiry grip I might have expected. His half-pie beard is surprisingly soft against my forehead. For some long time we just sit, side by side against the bedroom wall, under the First Fifteen.

Through a sort of sleep, propped against the wall, I hear his mother get up, make breakfast, and leave on foot for whatever her Saturday job is. She doesn't fuss or pry into the bedroom to see what's going on. Eventually Keith disengages, goes to shower, comes back dressed in white football gear, and asks about breakfast. I've no clothes to wear. His sister, the boy-mad handful who climbs through windows, is much smaller, he says. Eventually, I settle on a pair of his jeans, a thick woollen Swandri shirt, gloomy khaki; he produces socks and sandshoes which also fit my big feet. In the mirror I look sort of neuter.

'It's going to be wet. You'll need a mac', he says over a huge plate of weetbix and tinned peaches. 'My game's not till two, but I'm reffing a kids' game before, standing-in for a mate. Kids' games are fun.'

'Reffing?'

'Referee, hence the whites. Toast?'

'No.' The front of the *Herald* is telling me about rioting in the Congo and today the All Blacks play a game against Rhodesia which they are expected to win; the kitchen is freezing and needs a paint, even more than ours. 'Aren't you wondering ... what I'm doing here?'

He gets up to wash his weetbix plate. 'Nope. You'll tell me in your own good time.'

I climb into the blue Morris Minor feeling oddly detached from the memories it holds.

'You driving yet?' he says.

'Parents won't let me.'

'Quite right too.'

'You're one . . .' He's teasing. 'I thought you wrote this car off.'

'Mum and me bought another one.' You can't buy another face, you and that poor Vicki, I think, but I'm not in the mood to get into that. We're silent till we reach the car park outside the grounds. There's no chivalry here, no opening of car doors or umbrellas against the steady drizzle. He pulls his large bag of gear from the boot and throws me a thick brown oilskin.

'Keep dry. Here's a pound, to get in. I go thataway, you over there, that turnstile. See ya later, after my game, back here.' He's gone, long socks still white and snug around muscular calves.

'Thataway' means the players' entrance at the back of the tall and forbidding stands. He's right about one thing, today I want to be left alone, but I'm not quite sure how I ended up here of all places.

It's only when I join the men in the queue that I realize I'm wearing a sort of male uniform, and that no one is looking at me even once, let alone twice. I pay to go through the turnstile. On the field a boys' game is in progress, kids younger than Jamie, about ten. They look a bit like tiny Keystone cops, little feet twinkling often in the wrong direction, nowhere near the ball, until I realize there's nothing funny about the things that are being yelled at them from the sidelines.

'KICK the BALL, for God's sake. What's wrong with ya?' 'A bunch of pussy-cats.' 'A bunch of girls.' 'Put the boot in.' 'Pass, *pass*, PASS.' 'Jeez, the ref needs his head read.' 'Ya beauty,' as one little boy shakes himself free from twenty-nine other little boys and pounds off down the field. But mostly, it's instructions and abuse, while the drizzle pours steadily down, and the kids' hair and clothes get plastered to their little bodies.

It finishes, and Keith runs on to the field, sparkling white, brandishing his whistle, with thirty more boys, a bit older. The barrage of insults from the onlookers around the field — I suppose fathers, teachers, uncles, the odd hearty-voiced mum — begins again. The ground is now beginning to break up; Keith's whites are splattered with mud, and the kids are beginning to slip and slide about. It's so funny that I start to laugh for the first time in weeks.

Two men beside me under a huge black umbrella turn and stare. 'What's so funny?' one asks eventually, when the sight of a lone female laughing to herself becomes too much for him. There's just the slightest suggestion that if I don't stop I might get asked to move on, so I decide to go up into the stands.

If it's funny to see kids slithering around in the mud after a ball, it's anything but when Keith finally, after another schoolboys' game, runs on with his varsity team in blue and white and a team of very large men, mostly Maori, in maroon stripes. After half an hour, they are all varying degrees of mud-coloured, slipping and sliding round. Keith could be any one of the thirty. Every scrum that goes down I think of the sprigged boots on the kitchen table this morning, and dread the man at the bottom who won't, can't get up. A few punches are thrown; scrums threaten, but don't quite turn into brawls. This is the game the All Blacks think more important than the Maoris and those 150,000 people who signed the petition. I suppose the first Test they just lost over in Jo'berg last week in front of 75,000 spectators looked as ugly as this, without the mud. No one can run more than five yards without being mauled or slipping over, the forwards barge at each other like enraged bulls, the backs like fighting dogs. The whistle goes interminably. The ambulance men are called out at least ten times, three or four players get escorted or carried off, the crowd around me yells, hiccups, boos, groans, bellows, chants, cheers, hisses, complains, roars. I suppose the Colosseum in Rome sounded like this.

At half-time I can stand the noise and the blood and the violence no longer. I get up to leave. 'Make a good front-row forward,' I hear behind me, and a few male sniggers. I'm stupid enough to look: a row of louts clutching made-up dolls and beer bottles are there and it's me they're all grinning at.

'Great game,' says Keith when he joins me in the car a good hour later. His face is ruddy and shiny from the shower, and the scars have been joined by a big, swollen, purple bruise.

'Was it? Who won?'

'Weren't you there? It was on the scoreboard.'

'Nope. I decided I didn't like watching people stamp each other on the head.'

'Come on, this is Eden Park. The very ground where the All Blacks beat the Springboks four years ago. The game of the century. "Listen, Listen, It's a Goal".'

'So what.' He is looking round for the car keys. 'I've got them.'

He puts out his hand, then cocks his head when nothing happens.

'Don't play silly games, Alex.'

'Who's been doing just that! How can you go on playing if you're protesting against the tour?'

'Quite easily. I love the game, I hate apartheid. It's two *separare* issues. Now hand them over.'

In the enclosed space of the car I have smelt beer on his breath.

'No.' He puts his hands on the steering wheel and stares straight ahead.

'I've had one glass, that's all. The others are still in there at it.'

'So that makes you a hero?'

'I'm sober. Do I have to prove it by walking down that line on the road?'

'I'll drive.' Alex, you're a total fool. You don't have a licence and only five lessons from Dad under your belt.

'The keys.' He gets out of the car, and disdaining the rain wetting his dry clothes and dripping down his face, walks deliberately down a white parking line, one foot carefully after another; gives a sardonic old-fashioned bow. 'The keys.'

I'm too cold, I've no idea where to catch a bus and not enough money for a taxi, so I hand them over.

'Thank you,' he says, with heavy sarcasm. He drives sarcastically too, with elaborate stop signals, giving way where he doesn't have to, not more than 25 miles an hour.

'Where are we going?'

'Town. Want a milk shake? Or do you want to go home?'

'No.' We're outside a milk bar with the usual neon signs, juke box, next door to a pub. I might have known.

'I won't be long.'

'I've heard that before.'

'The team always meets here. I won't be longer than you getting a milk shake.'

'Prove it.'

'Pub closes at six anyway. Wait in the car.'

The creaming soda milk shake is the first substantial thing I'd had to eat all day. By the time it's finished I'm so angry I could throw the chairs around. How dare he, leave me here, while he gets boozed with his precious mates. I think of walking down to the pool, a bus home; letting his tyres down. Finally at ten to six I know there is a better solution.

The Public Bar is so crowded I have to push against the door. No one looks around as I elbow my way forward. They are all too damn busy getting as much beer down their ugly gullets before six. Despite the fuggy warmth of the place, there is nothing cosy about it; my wet sandshoes are on hard tiles, the walls are bare and painted a horrible pale green. Empty, it would be no more appealing than a public lavatory. The smell of beer, cigarettes and male sweat is overpowering, the noise presses on my head like a clamp. One man looks me straight in the eyes, registers surprise, shock, runs his eyes down what little he can see of my body, the boy's clothes don't go with the female face. Was I one of those skinny pansy boys with floppy wrists? I see him nudge his mate. It happens again, and again. I plough on regardless towards what must be the bar along the far side of the room. Keith, being on the short side, will be difficult to pick in this crush. By the time I see him, the place has gone quiet.

It is almost — almost — worth it for the look on his face as I push the last couple of yards. He is propping up the bar, a huge mug of beer in his hand, nearly full. I see shock and shame, and a flicker of regret as he puts his mug down on the bar.

'Hi,' I say finally.

'You're not allowed in here,' says a voice.

'Says who.'

'I say,' says the barkeeper, a squat tough character with a pock-marked face and piggy eyes. He has a sort of hose-pipe in his hand, filling up an unbelievable number of glasses in rows in front of him on the bar top. I'm surprised I remember all these details, but I do.

'Is there an actual law against women in bars?'

'Alex, we're going,' says Keith.

'Good. You said ten minutes.'

'On your way, girlie,' says the barkeeper.

'The missus wants you home, Keith old son,' mocks a voice. Keith is now pushing me, not with his hands because there's simply no room to put up a hand, but with his whole body. Body against body against body. I feel several wriggle and thrust against me as I am pushed towards the door. One deliberately blows a mouthful of smoke into my face, smiling as he does. Another rubs one of my short whisps of hair between his fat fingers. Another allows himself a long fruity belch, not quite in my face, but near enough.

But it is the smell I remember most, and the eyes which are mocking and merciless. Is this how Joan of Arc felt, surrounded by hostile angry men? And still the terrible silence until we are almost near the door and then the barkeeper delivers his punch line.

'Young tart. She should be ashamed of herself.'

The cold air hits me in the face. I am panting as though I'd just swum a hundred metre sprint, and my eyes are smarting from the smoke. So, I note, is Keith and his face behind the beard is a dark dusky red.

'God almighty, what ever possessed you, woman?'

'I don't like being kept waiting. You could have bought me a drink.'

He grips me by the shoulders. I think he is going to hit me, he is so angry. I notice I am, if anything, taller by two or three inches. Hit me Keith Jameson and you'll get it back with interest. 'Get this straight, you're under age as well as female, and you had no right ...'

'Under age, that's a laugh. So are you.' It's a stab in the dark, but I'm right.

'That's different.'

'Why? Because you play for Uni-varsity and engineering students think they're the bees knees.'

'I'm taking you home.'

'No you're not. Once was enough. How many jugs of that disgusting stuff have you had?'

He has me by the hand and is now pulling me along the street, around the corner. I am surprised at his strength. Several taxis are waiting at a rank and he propels me towards the first one, a big American tank.

'I'm taking you home.'

'No, please, I don't want to go home.'

'Why not?'

'None of your business.'

'It is my business when you choose my place to hide in.'

'I'm not hiding. Please, Keith,' I gasp, as he opens the taxi door with one hand, holding me firmly with the other. 'Please, please, don't, you're hurting, I can't ... go home, can't you see ...'

'Frankly no. Now get in.'

'No.' But he's too strong for me, when it comes to the point, and I'm pushed into the car. The seats are shiny and vast. I slither across, half on and half off the seat.

'Got a handful there mate,' says the taxi-driver sympathetically. I realize he is talking to Keith. 'Not nice to see a girl that age ...' He thinks I've been drinking.

'Half-wit!' I shout, 'It's him that's been ...'

'Shut up, Alex,' says Keith. 'I think it's time you told me what's going on.'

'Why bother, when you leave me to get pissed ...'

'Now look here ...' says the taxi-driver. 'I'm not obliged ...'

Keith interrupts, sharply. 'Please, that fish 'n' chip place half way up Queen Street.'

'A short fare,' grumbles the taxi-driver, but he pulls away from the rank, and negotiates the traffic coming in to the Saturday night pictures. Saved temporarily from the terrors of home, I run out of steam.

'You and I,' says Keith in a voice that brooks no nonsense, he'd make a good sergeant major, those officious eyebrows, 'are going to eat some fish 'n' chips, then we're going to the pictures. And hell, Alex, you're sexy when you're angry.'

The Saturday night pictures is one way to fill in the time with someone who may go off her rocker at any moment, but how could Keith have known what further torture he was putting me through. There am I, in my Swandri and borrowed men's jeans and muddy sandshoes, and there're all the couples, dressed up to the nines, the girls in their best coats and high heels, hair roller-set. The fish 'n' chips place isn't so bad, but at the cinema I skulk in the shadows, getting curious looks even there. Ironically it's *South Pacific*. By half-time I have stopped trembling and allowed him to hold my hand and agreed to go back to his place; his family will keep out of the way. We walk back up to the pub where he left the car. I'm grateful that he doesn't try to start a deep and meaningful conversation, and he drives normally. The house is quiet. He insists that I have his bed; he will sleep on the sofa; strangely, I trust him. Tomorrow, I think, as I drift into sleep surrounded by bridges, something significant might happen tomorrow. Today — if that's the way most men spend their Saturdays, at the footie and in the pub, they can have it.

I know the instant I wake, again at my normal time of five again wondering where the hell I am, what I have to do today; and it's not training because I seem to have lost my urge to swim every again, and it's not going home. It's the dream that tells me, the dream that has been haunting my nights; I have to find out what to do. Or can't do; the idea of peace, of shutting my tired eyes for ever ... why fight, for ever ...

Keith wanders in with the dawn.

'Mum and Jill won't wake for ages. Mum's only day off, she likes to sleep herself out. So,' he says, plonking himself on the end of the bed.

'Will you take me sailing this morning?'

'*Sailing?*'

'You offered, once.'

'That was summer. It's July. It'll be cold, looks like rain.'

'So. A little bit of rain.'

He grins, recognizing the echo, gets up and pulls back the curtains, revealing a grey sky, bare fruit trees bending to a good breeze. 'Marginal. And my boat needs a bit of work.'

'But nothing vital?'

'Suppose not. The gudgeon's a bit dicey,' he says, doubtfully.

'Scared? Too much wind?'

'Don't be daft.' But his eyes glint and I know he's taken the bait. 'Two up, we'll be fine.'

Dreamlike, I dress in my own clothes which I find washed and ironed on a chair, eat a piece of toast, help gather up oilskins, jumpers, sandwiches, the sail bags, the gear, and the boat itself on a trailer in the garden. The little Morris Minor makes heavy going of getting up the driveway.

It's the same beach and much the same wind as that other time, that other person.

'Twelve knots, at least,' says Keith, still dubious. The harbour looks grey and bleak; there's no one else out sailing, and only a couple of elderly women, well wrapped up, taking a Sunday morning walk along the beach. The tide is dead low, so we have to haul the trailer a long way down to the shallows. Keith takes an age to rig the boat; all the shackles are a bit stiff, he says. I'm cold already. My jeans are wet to the knees.

'Right. Where are we going?' says Keith, looking out at the choppy, murky green sea. In shorts and bare legs sticking out from bulky oilskins he looks top heavy. 'You'd have been better with shorts. Hop in. Or do you want to sail her?'

'Later.'

We get sorted out remarkably quickly and head up harbour towards the naval base. Even that has its memories, every place I turn.

'It's going to be a short sail.'

'Why?'

'Look at the sky.' It's overcast, but over the distant western hills is an ominous cloud, deep grey and menacing. Already the waves are breaking against the side of the hull and against our protruding backsides.

'Can I steer?'

He hesitates. 'First time?'

'No,' I lie. Andy had not suggested that I steer.

'I've steered before,' I say impatiently.

'OK. Slide behind me, take the tiller, give me the jibsheet, I'll keep the mainsheet.'

'What do I aim for?'

'Sail her full and bye.'

'What?' I have the tiller, we are sitting very close on the left rail and the sails are flapping wildly.

'See the sail lifting by the mast? Bear away to starboard a bit.

You're too close to the wind, sail on the main.'

I haven't the slightest idea what he is talking about, but I do something with the tiller and magically the sails stretch and curve and we take off like the clappers.

'That's it!'

I find I can hold her steady.

'We're really on a tight reach. Point her up a bit, towards the bridge,' says Keith. 'No, the other way.'

Damn and damn, speak English man! But the speed is fantastic; this is living dangerously; this is what I wanted; this is my dream. I see Keith looking over his shoulder at the approaching wall of grey.

'We should go back,' he shouts.

'Why? I like it. I want to sail under the bridge. You can tell me all about it.'

'It's too far. That squall . . .'

'A little squall.'

'There's twenty knots of wind in that squall,' he shouts. 'At least. Put her about.'

'I want to sail under the bridge.'

'Christ, Alex, do as you're bloody told.' He grabs the tiller and pushes it away. There's a large amount of noise and scrambling, ropes everywhere; he flings himself across the other side, but somehow we make it on to the other tack, pointing towards the cargo ships and tall cranes of the city wharves. I'm still in control of the tiller.

'We're going back.'

'Let's put the spinnaker up.'

'Don't be bloody silly.'

'Too much wind for Keithy-baby?'

He doesn't bother to respond. 'You'd better let me take her.'

'Why? I'm doing OK.'

'We've got to run off back to the beach.'

'Running away from a bit of wind.' But even as I shout, a gust catches the sails and lays us on our ear. Keith flings himself almost off the boat; the mainsail flaps; we straighten up a bit. There was rain in that gust as well as power and beyond the cranes the city has disappeared. I'm soaked, teeth literally chattering, every part of me vibrating.

'I want to take her.' There's panic in his voice, and I feel him start to push behind me.

'*Move!*'

'I'm OK.'

'You are not OK — and here's another one. Watch it. *Bring her up.*'

'What the hell does that mean?' But this time the gust is stronger again and though he moves fast, he's too late. The boom is already in the water, and I hear something crack sharply like a gun going off. 'Oh Christ.'

I'm caught off balance. I fall forward, downwards into the sea, tangled with the mainsheet. The water down here is sort of khaki green, I think. It's quite warm. I have a rope around my neck.

I am going to die.

Isn't that what I want?

The rope gets tighter. Now I've managed to get my fingers around wire, rope, something, trying to pull them away from my clothes, my body, my neck, but although I'm kicking my legs like fury to get to the surface, nothing is happening. This is how a fish feels in a net, a person grappling with a giant octopus. This is where I always wake up. This is why I bullied Keith to bring me sailing and why I probably hoped that the boat would somehow capsize, who will ever know, although something broke, I heard it . . .

I'm weightless and calm. Oh well, I think, a certain irony, on a number of counts. Serve you right, Keith old son, drowning me successfully where you failed to mangle me in your car last year; and Andy old son, making me get back in your boat because I felt sorry for you and in those days life was worth living. But that day I was never in danger, I have never been in danger, not real mortal *danger*, and now I am; and one third of me is saying that life has not proved worth living without you, and another third is saying that you weren't the strong person I believed you to be, and I'm tired of fighting you and everyone else who wants to tame me and I want some peace; and the last third is saying that I'd be a bloody fool and coward to sink to the bottom of the Waitemata Harbour here and now and let my enemies gloat — and I'm still struggling against the wire, the ropes, the heavy clothes holding me down, and my lungs are beginning to demand that they get some air from somewhere, otherwise it will be water that floods in, and curtains for Alex Archer.

In my dream this is where I wake up.

In my dream I'm in a frenzy. But now I'm resigned, *che sera sera*. Was this what I had always known? That teacher in intermediate school, remember? She said one in four of us sitting in the classroom that day would not reach the age of twenty, and we had all looked furtively around and firmly told Destiny to lay his sticky paws on cross-eyed Jocelyn over here, or that nasty lad Kevin at the back, or that tell-tale Sally with the nits in her hair ... but it was me all along.

*I am not ready*!

Dammit, despite everything, I have unfinished business and scores to settle and I'm bloody well *not ready*.

My hands are grabbing wood, rope, something smooth, the sail, desperately now. Oh God, help me. Why should he? He didn't help Andy. My head is pounding, oh I don't want that khaki water in my lungs ...

When I have to breathe in something, it's air I breathe, a great, gasping, spluttering, salty, beautiful lungful.

There are hills over there, and there, and waves and spray, and it's pouring black driving rain. The hull of the boat is high above me, and I'm trying to hold on to a tangle of ropes, finding out that being an Olympic swimmer is no guarantee that three wet woollen jumpers won't drag you down into the green murk, and there's no sign of Keith. I cough some more, and kick my feet like fury to stay afloat, and then a head surfaces near me and we look at each other.

'Jesus, Alex,' says a spluttering voice. 'Oh, Jesus, I thought you were a goner.'

He swims around to the stern, holds out a hand and pulls me over towards the hull. I hang on and splutter up water.

'Hang on tight. I couldn't find you, I thought ...' What about the three people you put in hospital after Helensville; or me popping up as a bloated corpse in two days' time, think about those. His free hand is pushing the hair off my forehead in a most strange manner. Then he heaves himself over and kisses me hard on the mouth. I taste salt, I feel his beard, the pressure of his teeth hard against mine.

'Get off,' I gasp, with only one hand available to do any pushing off, especially if he thinks I'm going to open my mouth. 'They say you're randy but this is ridic ...'

'Who does?'

'Girls at school.'

He smiles, and his gnomish face with its scraggy eyebrows and mangy beard, scars and footie bruise looks strangely gentle.

'That, my friend, was a kiss of thanks be to God.' He finds a better handgrip on the smooth wood of the hull. It's crunch time. 'Now tell me, what's wrong at home?'

'Nothing's wrong at home.'

'Then why ...?'

'I had to get ... my trip to Rome's under a wee cloud.'

'But you're going next month.'

'Possibly.' I have a coughing fit, tasting salt.

He gives a disbelieving laugh. The rain beats down harder still. It's a funny place for a tête-à-tête.

'That's not it.'

'Meaning?'

'It's time you got Andy out of your system.'

'I have.'

'So a picture of the First Fifteen sets you off? Look, he was my mate, I miss him like hell, the bloody waste ...'

'You could do the same, knock someone down any time, the way you drive ...'

'You don't give an inch, do you?'

'Yeah, well, isn't it about time we got this boat up and sailed home?'

'We can't. The gudgeon went. And I forgot the oars.'

'So what happens now?'

'We wait. A ferry just left from Devonport. We'll signal. And you're going to listen. Why do you think Andy wanted to go to Dartmouth?'

I thought that was my special secret? He coughs and spits up water and gets a firmer handhold to deliver his broadside.

'Sure, he liked the idea of the navy. Secure job, travel, glamour, smart uniform.'

'Not fair. It was the sea ...'

'It was also to get as far away as possible from his old man. Nothing was ever good enough. His marks. Girlfriends. They thought he should have been Head Boy, not just a prefect.'

I'm silent; he grabs at the hull again.

'You thought, just a pompous but basically kind old gent. I tell you, he had those two underfoot.'

'His mother, yes.'

'And Andy. The night he died ...'

'It was something on at school.'

'Not the whole story. We had our last exam that day, remember? We should have been celebrating, but he turned up at school looking like death warmed up. He told me his old man had started on at tea about him going to med' school. Wouldn't listen to any overtures about the navy. Pompous old sod. "We'll discuss it later, Andrew." So basically he was terrified to go home, hung about being a good boy helping the caretaker, *that's* why he was pedalling home at midnight and copped it.'

'Mr Richmond said it was eleven.'

'It was midnight,' Keith yells, spluttering. 'And if that old bastard doesn't know why ...'

The ferry motors past towards town, hard going against the driving wind and waves. Keith and driver exchange signals and we are close enough to see him talk into a microphone. Calling Coastguard.

I have never been colder in my life. I've even stopped shivering. I can't quite shape the words I'm looking for.

'Look,' says Keith. 'You and Andy might have made a go of it. I doubt it. He wasn't strong enough for you.'

I hear an echo of Mr Richmond when I visited them on Christmas Day. *You'd have been good for him.* How bloody ironic.

'Anything else ... tell me, that I should know?' I say.

'I'll talk about Andy any time you want. How the Third Formers worshipped him at school, six-foot, good-looking, in all the right teams. How he knew it, played on it. How he was hopeless with money. How he let people ride over him, too damn polite, you too. How he tried everything to get rid of that stutter, hypnosis even, because in the end you can't have naval officers who stutter.'

'No more,' I say, weeping freely at last for the person I only half knew. 'Stop it.'

He gets a fresh grip on the boat, but this time one of his deathly white hands is covering mine and I'm grateful.

'He was my mate too,' he says and there's a catch in his voice which I know is not from the salty grey waves surrounding us.

---

I suppose it was about ten minutes before a small white launch slowly motored alongside, and by then both of us were paralysed purple and even yellow with cold. Keith, with little help from me, had managed to get the boat upright, and the sails down, and we were both concentrating on simply hanging on to the side. The worst of the squall had passed. Two men peered down.

'Who's in the best shape?' one shouted.

'Me,' said Keith and he was right.

'We'll take the other chap aboard. You got a painter there?'

A rope came over, with a loop which went underneath my armpits. That was difficult enough, with oilskins and all, and it took both of them to haul me aboard because I had no strength to help myself and the waves made things difficult. 'Crazy kids, this weather, not a lifejacket in sight,' one grumbled. He had an English accent and looked like the bearded sailor on the de Reske cigarette packet. It appeared that we had interrupted them doing a spot of fishing.

I stood dripping on to his carpet and just looked at him.

'Get your clothes off, lad,' he said impatiently. 'Dennis, this kid's in a pretty bad way. How's the other one?' His mate was leaning over the side talking to Keith.

'Managing, just.'

'Young idiots. Come on, get them off.' All was slow motion, he helped me with oilskin and jumpers, while my personal devil, amused that for the second time in two days I'd been mistaken for a boy, waited for the moment when I got down to my bra. I wrapped the towel around myself before taking my bra off, and gave him a weak smile.

'Humblest apologies, miss. Just goes to show — I thought only some damn fool boys would be stupid enough to be out in the harbour today.'

'All in a good cause,' I said, feeling rather sleepy as he wrapped the blankets around me.

'I can't imagine what. Now curl up on that bunk and conserve what little body heat you've got. We'll have you ashore soon. Eat this.' He handed me some sort of chocolate bar, which I attacked greedily, because it was well past lunch-time and I'd had no proper food for two days.

'Your face is familiar.'

'No.'

'Funny. What's your name?'

'Alice. Alice Archibald.'

'Tom?' called the other one from outside. 'You free?'

'Coming.' So we rocked around on the harbour, and I'm ashamed to say I drifted off to sleep while poor Keith also got hauled aboard and they stripped him down too, and put him on the other bunk — and thus we made our ignominious way home.

Worse was in store. Through a state of half sleep, I heard a lot of business with bringing the launch into the jetty, and doing whatever had to be done to Keith's sad-looking Cherub. An ambulance was waiting, with a burly uniformed driver who came aboard and told us we were going to hospital to be kept under observation for hypothermia, whatever that was, whereupon I raised a great stink and told him we were perfectly all right and I wanted to go home where my mother was a nurse and could handle anything; so he checked us over and said we seemed to be a couple of fit young people and all right, he'd take us home.

Of the two evils, Mum's wrath, or the hospital where I'd almost certainly be recognized and have to give my name (thus the Press might get wind of Olympic swimmer admitted for observation after near drowning in sailing accident) — Mum was just slightly preferable.

Only just. Keith was provided with some of Dad's spare clothes and put in the car and driven home by Dad. Later I heard he'd got the rough end of Dad's tongue about taking me sailing, with the risk of injury and so forth.

As for me, I was put to bed, given scrambled eggs to eat.

Everyone talked softly as though I was sick, just recovering from an operation or something. No questions or explanations were demanded, which was bizarre.

Mr Jack was summoned.

After the pleasantries, we all sat and looked at each other in the firelight. The kids had been shooed off to bed, Gran was doing some hand sewing on some fine lemon-yellow cotton and Mum was smoking and knitting furiously. The battle lines were drawn, but no one wanted to fire the first arrow.

'Well, Miss Alice Archibald,' said Mum finally. 'We know this much. You've been with Keith. You stayed at his house. You went to watch a football match yesterday, and to the pictures last night. This morning you went sailing and nearly drowned yourselves.'

'That's about right,' I said, sure as hell not about to fill in the gaps. 'How do you know?'

'His mother rang us Friday night.'

'Oh, did she.'

'There are *some* responsible people around, Alex.'

'Helena,' said Dad sharply.

'Put it this way,' said Mum. 'We haven't been worrying unduly about you.'

Mr Jack saw my disbelieving smirk.

'It's true, Alex,' he said. 'I've had two whole mornings in bed, snoozing till seven.'

He shifted forward in his armchair. Here it comes, I thought.

'Something had to give. Are we back in business, Alex? Or are we going to put an end to it? Withdraw you from the team. I'll ring Cyril Upjohn tonight. Now. One phone call. That's all it will take.'

If it was shock tactics, it worked.

'What!'

'Don't say ...' began Mum automatically.

'You couldn't.'

'I could,' he said and it was my eyes which dropped first. There was a long, long silence.

'I wasn't born yesterday, Alex,' he said gently. 'I know about the letter, and what happened at the wedding. I know you went into a public bar last night ...'

'For God's sake,' said Mum, using her strongest oath. 'This is going from bad to worse.'

'How?' I said, conscious of a dark flush seeping upwards.

'A mate of mine — not your Keith — happened to be in there and rang me. He said you looked — fairly desperate. And you got a rough ride. True?'

I had closed my eyes against the memory. You could do nothing private in this bloody country.

'This Keith,' said Mr Jack gently. 'I don't know him.'

'He's all right,' I mumbled.

Mum interrupted sharply. 'I don't agree. That potentially disastrous trip to Helensville. Car crashes. Protest marches. As for going sailing midwinter, an act of irresponsible lunacy. He's not all right.'

'I got out of his car, didn't I?'

'What are you talking about, Alex?' Oh hell, Mr Jack never knew about that little incident, how close I'd come to disaster.

'I went marching because I believed in it.' They looked unimpressed. I took a deep breath. 'All right then, the sailing was my idea. I bullied him into it.'

'Why?' said Mr Jack, fixing me with a gentle smile. 'Hoping for an injury, an excuse not to train? Going with a friend of Andy's as a means of getting closer to him? Putting yourself at extreme risk ...'

'Dinghy sailing is not extreme risk,' I said loftily. 'Thousands of people do it.'

'Given certain conditions, it could turn out that way. It nearly did.' He didn't need to say the obvious next line: is that what you wanted? Nor the answer: yes. I mean no. Well perhaps I ... *No!* He sat back in his chair.

Tears were spilling down my cheeks, splashing on to my hands. I had just enough stuffing left in me to leave; not angrily; but slowly, sadly, suddenly very tired, empty.

There's a knock on the door.

'Go away.'

'Alex? I'd like to come in.'

The door opens slowly and Mr Jack walks in. He sits down heavily on top of the assorted bras, jumpers, old jeans, damp towels on the one chair. He makes no sign that the mess and the smell are rather bad. He sits there, on the edge of the chair, his two squat legs firmly planted in front of him, his pudgy fingers interlaced, thumbs going round and round. And then he tells me about the long drawn-out business of watching his mother die.

I notice how much weight he's lost, the deeper lines on his face. I've forgotten that he is grieving too. Those weeks without him — how petty my fights with Steve seem now.

'My sister didn't miss a chance to point out she'd been looking after mother for years. Then there've been arguments over the sort of funeral, the family furniture. I'm betting on problems with the will. I'm wishing now I'd taken Lorna over with me, at least try to mend a few fences.'

I remember what Mrs Jack had hinted at the airport.

'People say, sorry about your mother, Bill, know how you feel, and it makes me hopping mad, because how can they ever *know*. How can *I* know what you've been going through? I can't.'

There's a hush in the room.

'But then I get back and see you choosing to destroy yourself, it's more than I can cope with. My old Mum had had a good innings, but she had no control over her situation, none whatsoever. From the day they put her on oxygen, pain and hallucinations till the day she finally went. But you have.'

I am crying again.

'I think — something happened this weekend. Some sort of decision? Perhaps you don't quite recognize it as such, yet. I'm not asking you to tell me, except ... Am I right?'

I nod.

Then I say, 'When we capsized today, I thought I wasn't going to come up. I didn't want to ...'

He picks his way through the shambles on the floor, leans down and very delicately kisses my forehead.

'It won't all happen at once. We'll still have our bad days, you and me. But it's going to be all right, champ.'

*Part Four*

I HAVE decided to keep a diary, from now on; only five weeks before we go, Rome and all that. Mum says when I'm fifty I'll be jolly glad I did, to have something to show my grandchildren! So Gran rushed out and bought me a special sort of notebook, with a hard green cover. My Trip Book.

> **July 4 1960.** Hullo Diary, good to know you. Actually enjoyed training today for the first time in ages. Only two days off — but it seemed like two weeks, two months, as though I'd been on holiday. Mr Jack has drawn up a new schedule — more medleys, to stop boredom setting in. He wants me to go for runs as well, and do more calisthenics and weights if I can stand it. Now, I can. Had postcard from Maggie in Queensland — she's due back in three weeks, lucky bitch, all that sparkling blue water. Mr Jack's heard rumours about the coaches there, that they don't get on, they train separately, spy on each other's squads, rows even, pathetic. Funny, I'm not worried about Maggie now — we're both going, we'll both do our best. Liar, I want to do better than her. Have enjoyed the break from Mrs B. Something on the postcard about a fashion parade at her school on the 28th. I remember some woman ringing weeks ago, something about some special bathing-suits from somewhere, me and Maggie, anyway, saying no. Perhaps it might be quite fun. And poops to all those rumours.
>
> Keith rang tonight, to see how I was! He's got a derrible cold in the dose. I felt rather bad about that, for a while. But under that gruff exterior ... hope he doesn't get all randy and boring. Not that I need worry, really, he hasn't asked me out and I haven't got time or energy even if he did. Maybe just once? Perhaps later, after Rome?!
>
> Riding to school this morning, I saw the first blossom out — pink blossom in the rain. I stopped just to look up close. I feel — is this corny, diary? — I'm seeing everything fresh, sharp, clean, as though a big weight has been lifted off my chest. Mr Jack is going to have a chat to Mr Upjohn, tell him about The New Look Alex. Toeing the party line and all that. Well, not so long to go now.

**July 6.** Bad news. Mr Jack once said he might have enough money saved to go to Rome. If I'd stopped to think about it, I should have guessed he'd used it all up going to Sydney. And he got a letter from the solicitor today to say that his sister's family are contesting the will and it's all held up, at least a year, so there's no hope of money there. His winter job doesn't bring in all that much, not enough to persuade the bank manager for a loan. When he told me, I made all sorts of silly suggestions about Mrs J. getting a job, and persuading the swimming association that we should have an official coach and he said fat chance of that, Alex; there are already two swimming officials for two swimmers. Funny really, I don't know why Mrs Churchill couldn't have been both manager and chaperon, (leave Mr Upjohn behind!) but Mr Jack says managers are always men and I don't see why a woman couldn't be a manager just as well.

**July 8.** Mr Upjohn came down to early morning training today the first time ever. Said he'd had a very useful chat with Mr Jack, and how was I feeling Alex? — fine, fine — and he was very much looking forward to setting off on our great adventure together. I guess it's a case, if you can't beat her, join her. He was so nice I began to wonder if what I overheard in Napier and the two letters had all been a bad dream, figment of my imagination.

**July 9.** We marked the Trial Scene for *Joan* at school today. We've done readings in class and I knew most of the lines, but it was really creepy; even surrounded by a lot of fat schoolgirls trying to be the Bishop and the Inquisitor and things, the words are so wonderful, so musical, so powerful it doesn't really matter who says them, and I felt just like I did in that pub, totally alone, daring to be yourself, different, surrounded by hostility. And then a very strange thing happened. When we got to the speech where Joan tells them to go take a running jump, the words are so beautiful and strong and defiant, something sort of took over. *Light your fire: do you think I dread it as much as the life of a rat in a hole? My voices were right.* I know Joan was talking about something much more important, like what she believes and how terrible it would be to be shut away in a prison breathing foul damp darkness for ever, but, well, it's an amazing cry for freedom and life and it just came out and when I finished the girls who were supposed to shout 'Blasphemy, She is possessed, Monstrous' and so on, just stood there looking stupid. There was a bit of an awkward pause and I felt a bit stupid myself because it was only a rehearsal and there's nothing worse than people overacting. But Miss Macrae stopped the lesson, and told the others it was time for a break which it wasn't, and told me to stay behind, and came slowly over to me and I believe her eyes were a bit moist. *Tears*, her of the plain suits and voice like a foghorn.

'I once swore, many moons ago, I'd never hear those words spoken on a stage again.' Something held me back from asking why. She'd tell me if she wanted to. But she only said 'Thank you Alex', wiping her eyes. I didn't know where to look.

'I suppose you have to do law?' and I said I did, with more conviction than I ever felt before.

Then quite on impulse, out of nowhere, I said, 'Julia says, it won't do my reputation any good, playing Joan,' and she gave me a long penetrating stare and then she started to smile.

'Julia really should know better, such nonsense,' she said, but kindly and then the bell rang. 'You will be a magnificent Joan.'

---

Maggie rang the day she got back from Queensland. She was fed up with Aussies lording it over her and scrapping among themselves, though Dawn Fraser was just amazing and actually talked to her several times like a real person, not a kid from New Zealand, and asked about her times and everything, and she'd even heard about you, Alex, really, and said she looked forward to meeting you in Rome.

I asked about the boyfriend she met last year. He hadn't made the Aussie team, she said sadly; it had all fizzled out, and he'd gone back to Perth which was over the other side of the entire continent. She was really, really glad to be home, even though it meant another two weeks' training with eyes out on stalks, and she had some fabulous Aussie clothes to show me. Her Mum had really gone to town in Sydney on the way home. You've picked up an Aussie accent, Maggie, I said — Seedney, listen to you; yes, Mum's working on it, she laughed.

It was a long phone call, because she seemed really keen to tell me everything and to hear what I'd been up to — nothing much, I said, just training, and more training, and my eyes were pretty bad but otherwise the last few weeks had been OK 'cause now it was close enough to believe we were actually going, and Mr Jack was beginning to cut back my miles slightly which was a relief. Letters had started appearing in the mail about travel plans and inoculations and being measured for uniforms and assembling in Auckland on August 9 — two weeks, fantastic wasn't it, incredible, can't believe it? Not forgetting boring old school, I said, getting so behind with my homework it wasn't funny, but the teachers were being pretty soft. I could do without all the sniggering about Italian boys and bottom pinching, and endlessly telling people of our stopovers — Sydney, Darwin, Singapore, Calcutta, Karachi, Beirut, Cairo, Rome, gosh, lucky you, they all gasp; tedi-ous, I said. She said she wasn't going back to school before we go — there was no point really — but, she said, there's this woman called Mrs Sutherland who rang two minutes after they got back, wanting to know if she and I could *possibly*; she knew it was asking a great deal of us, only two weeks before we go away; but *could* we possibly come over to Maggie's school on Friday afternoon and wear these fabulous American bathing-suits for her fashion parade. It was in such a good cause, the Crippled Children's Society, and she would just *love* to be able to send around a notice from school tomorrow saying that our two very own Olympic girl swimmers would model these beautiful garments. Honestly, Alex, she did go on and on, said Maggie. 'In the end I said I had to ask you.'

'What does your mother say?' I said.

'She ... strange really, she vaguely thought no harm in it, but I'd feel such an idiot, prancing round in those things. I don't want to. You'd be all right.'

'I've never modelled anything in my life.'

'Mum wasn't all that interested, she's rushing round, packing, getting tickets and everything. You know her and Dad are coming too.'

'I heard,' I said sourly. I had no proof that it was Mrs B who tattled on me about the wedding, but it figured and I intended to be as cold as a cucumber to her from now on. 'Oh, what the hell Maggie, a bit of fun. Ring the woman.'

Oh, Alex, you fool!

I didn't actually see Maggie until the Friday morning, because not being at school, she was able to train at civilized hours during the day, almost as though she was doing it for a job. Well, the Aussies are at training camps, and Maggie doesn't have to work 'cause she's got rich parents, I suppose one day there will be swimmers and athletes doing it as a job, being paid by the Government, perhaps, or getting prizes for winning, enough to live on. It's a strange thought.

Mrs Sutherland kept ringing me up, and I suppose Maggie too. I was a size 14, wasn't I? but the company supplying the garments were sending both 12s and 14s, so there'd be one that should fit. Could I bring a pair of white shoes with highish heels, 'cause bathing-suits always look so much better with shoes on, don't they. No, I couldn't and wouldn't, I said. But in beauty contests they always . . . that's beauty contests, I said, I'm sorry Mrs Sutherland but if you want me you'll have me in bare feet or not at all. There was a stunned silence. Game, set and match to me, I thought, easy really. I'm getting wise to bullies in my old age.

I didn't actually tell my family what I was up to, except that I was going to Maggie's school to talk to juniors about going to the Games. Perhaps I was a bit bashful, unwilling to have the kids jumping round teasing me about being a model and walking like Marilyn Monroe, and would they have to pad my bosoms 'cause I wouldn't be able to fill them up by myself. I don't know, anyway, it was a mistake. Maggie and I were due at her school for a trial run about ten, so we both went training an hour later than my usual, and for the first time we actually trained together. Her coach had got the huff about her going to Australia, and so she's working to her Australian coach's schedules again. Mrs B didn't come into the pool. We compared our schedules and found they were quite similar, so we swam together and did some time trials together.

It was so wonderful having someone alongside to pace me, I wished we'd trained together a long time ago.

In the changing-room afterwards I heard a sharp intake of breath. I turned from doing my jeans up to find Maggie sitting on the bench, bent over, looking rather odd.

'What's the matter?'

'Nothing. Just the gripes.'

'Period?'

'Last week.'

'Nerves about this afternoon, I bet.'

'Oh, sure. I wish I'd said no.'

'Maggie, are you all right?'

She slowly resumed getting dressed. 'I had it once or twice in Aussie. It'll go. Mum says it'll go and it always does, with an aspirin or two.'

'My Mum says any pain in the gut should be investigated.'

'No, it's all right, truly.'

If I were her, I'd be dead scared about appendicitis too, right now. But she said it had gone, and I believed her.

I had never actually been in Maggie's school, which was grand and brick, with wonderful trees all round. I had managed to say hullo and goodbye to Mrs B, driving us there in her Super Snipe, without actually looking her in the eye. Mrs Sutherland was all over us like a rash. The togs were hanging on a rack in a classroom backstage, and we both gaped at creations of lycra and net and Grecian drapes and South Sea Island prints, ruches and tucks and insets and skirts. One or two were okay, I suppose, but I thought most of them horrendous and wished with all my heart that we had not got ourselves into this.

There was a large amount of talk and carry-on, clipboards at the ready, and girls parading round in their suits and dresses made in dressmaking class. It appeared Maggie and I were to wear ten garments each; some mothers would be on hand to help us change quickly. We tried each of the ten on, resulting in a lot more discussion about the absolute necessity of padding the cups with cotton wool (I reluctantly had to agree), accessories, bags and straw hats and beachcoats and jewellery until I could have screamed. Walking down the catwalk was rather strange. I'm used to standing on starting-blocks in front of three thousand people; walking down a school hall in the bikini which was the climax of the swim-suit bit left me feeling very exposed.

Lunch-time came, and I wanted to go home, but Mrs Sutherland had thoughtfully organized lunch. The parade started at one thirty, so we could rest in the senior common room until we were called. The senior common room was like a railway station, because half the senior school wanted to come and see their mate Maggie back for the day and wish her luck for Rome and also cast an eye over her notorious friend from that other school. After about twenty minutes of that, I knew I had to go for a walk or blow up. Maggie was looking decidedly pale and said she'd stay, you go Alex, don't forget to come back, she called.

Well, I walked around the grounds for a bit and went back inside at one o'clock as I was asked.

'Where's Maggie?' I asked Mrs Sutherland.

'I'm sorry, Alex, she's gone home.'

'Gone *home*?'

'Her mother insisted that she wasn't well. I tried Alex, oh dear, we'll just have to make the best of it, won't we. I've got a Sixth Former to wear Maggie's costumes, but it won't be the same, will it?'

'Thanks a bundle,' I said. But because I knew about her stomach-ache this morning, I believed it to be true, and I feared it might be appendicitis. I knew that I had to go through this terrible farce alone. Had to? I could have walked away, but I'm not a quitter. It was for a good cause.

Images and memories now go hazy around the edges.

I do remember another argument with Mrs Sutherland over make-up. The Sixth Former was so thrilled with being Maggie's stand-in and actually modelling a bikini, showing off her body beautiful to the assembled hall of parents and teachers and pupils gathered to raise money for the Crippled Children, that she allowed Mrs Sutherland's sidekick to go overboard. I took one look at the pancake, precise eyebrows, and heavy black lines drawn around her eyes for the latest Vogue doe-eyed look and flipped.

'You can forget that stuff,' I said.

'The lights . . .' began the woman, damp sponge and paintbrush at the ready.

'Not on your nellie.' So Mrs Sutherland was called over and we had another row and she danced up and down, a little plump pudding on her high heels, and told me I was being quite neurotic, and I said I'm here, Mrs Sutherland, I'll wear your bathing-costumes for the Crippled Children but I'll not look like a tart of twenty-five for anyone; whereupon, the Sixth Former danced around a bit too, in her first costume of gold lamé in Grecian mode, and called me a few names. Mrs Sutherland burst into copious tears and made me feel a total heel, because it's a terrible thing to see an adult who hasn't got a clue how to handle people, totally out of her depth. So we reached a compromise — I put on a bit of make-up and combed my hair into a sort of Audrey Hepburn pixie look, while the sidekick stood and sneered, and the parade began only fifteen minutes late.

The bathing-suit bit came at the end, after wall-to-wall teenage fashion, introduced by the honeyed tones of Mrs Sutherland in her best black compere's dress, while the dressmaking teacher fussed over each petrified girl as she waited behind the curtains for her name. Then it was our turn, the Sixth Former in stilettos you could kill someone with at twenty paces, and me in my bare feet sporting bosoms I never knew I had. Please welcome our Olympic girl, Alex Archer, who has kindly consented to join us today, and so forth. We got lots of claps and gasps when the bikinis appeared; you had to be *very* daring to wear a bikini as brief as these, showing your navel.

I was vaguely aware of hearing the brand name mentioned in the commentary; a tiny alarm bell started ringing. I was not aware (because of the coloured spotlights that some father was training right into our eyes, and the general confusion of music and applause) of a photographer taking pictures without flash, with an extra fast film. I should have been.

I rang Maggie that night after training to see how she was. It was a rather confused conversation. She was fine, the pain had gone; so why had she run away and left me, at *her* school too. She hedged a bit, and then told me her mother had changed her mind about allowing her to model swim-suits, but she thought it was more tactful to tell Mrs Sutherland she wasn't well. I suppose she said it was cheap, or something like that, I said, and Maggie laughed with surprise; how did you know? I know your mother, I said. Anyway, it was over, and they'd raised a hundred and fifty pounds for the Crippled Children, and Mrs Sutherland was over the moon.

The weekend passed uneventfully — just Gran ironing, yet again, all the cotton clothes she had made, and Mum getting the best family suitcase out of the hall cupboard, and more letters arriving to tell us about team meetings and photos to be taken in the domain, and booklets about Rome. The All Blacks had won another game in South Africa.

---

Monday morning, the first day of August, our Olympic world begins to fall apart.

I come home from school to find Gran has taken a message from Mr Jack. Would I be prepared to stay on after training tonight, please, for an appointment with Mr Upjohn?

'What does he want,' I ask before I start training. Mr Jack doesn't know either, but he didn't like the tone of Mr Upjohn's voice when he rang. I assume, he says, there's nothing you're hiding from me? Only Maggie's stomach-ache, I think naïvely, and that's not really my problem and it's probably not a problem at all, just nerves, tension.

Mr Upjohn arrives wearing his new black New Zealand Olympic blazer, with Rome 1960 on the pocket, and there's trouble writ large all over him. I'm still in my old track suit, and feeling rather cold. He marches down the concourse and over to where we are standing, and launches his rocket.

'Can you explain this?' he says, fumbling with the flaps of a large brown envelope. He holds up a photograph. Mr Jack and I stare at it.

'Well?'

Mr Jack sits down heavily on the form where he has sat for two winters watching me train. I know what he is thinking: six years, blown. Vanity, ah vanity, all is vanity.

'Well?' Mr Upjohn says impatiently. 'I'm waiting.'

The look I get from Mr Jack wounds me more than any words could. Reproach, incredulilty, resignation — he raises his hands and drops them as if to say, 'I give up'.

'Do you realize what you've done, Alex?' Mr Upjohn demands. 'Do you realize the implications of this? Wasn't the last warning enough? Don't you realize, child?'

I'm beginning to. But I cannot speak, because I'm burning fire all over as I look at what seems to be a press photograph, eight by six. Two girls simper out of it. One is rather glamorous, posing as in cheesecake, high heels, a brief bikini; under the bright lights, the doe-eyed look didn't look too bad. The other is, though barefoot, taller, slimmer, less posed, amateurish, rather bored. Me.

I take it, stupidly. The name and address of a photographer is stamped on the back, and a slip of paper has been pasted. 'Alex Archer (left) teenage swimming champion and Olympic hopeful, appeared at a charity fashion parade in Auckland last week. The glamorous swim-suits are by Rose Marie of California.'

'How in the name of heaven has this arrived in my office, Alex?' My silence is getting to him. 'Well? Have you nothing to say for yourself?'

'Not much, 'cause you won't believe me, anyway.'

'We'll ignore that.'

'I didn't see a photographer. I wasn't asked about photographers, no one warned me, no one told me, no one said anything about the Press.'

'Haven't you learned by now, Alex, that *everything* you do is potential news?' says Mr Upjohn.

'It was only a school thing. Last Friday, at Maggie's school. Some stupid parade, their dressmaking teacher and some jumped-up parent who saw herself as a fashion co-ordinator. Maggie and I ...'

'Maggie too?' He gulps. 'You can't be serious.'

'I am, though her silly bitch of a mother changed her mind and took her away at the last minute and left me in the lurch.'

'Alex, you will show some respect ...'

'Why? She hates me, it's mutual.'

'At least she had some sense about this — this *charade*.'

That's strange, I'm thinking. Why did she? Had she worked out that any picture of me or Maggie in someone's bathing-suits could be seen as advertising? Could get us wiped out of the Games team, no longer true amateurs. Maggie was putting all that on, about a pain in her guts? I don't believe it. I know you too well, Maggie Benton. Do I? The devilishness of the idea is too much. I subside on to the form next to Mr Jack.

Mr Upjohn is relentless. 'Look at you, baring your midriff to the world.'

'You mean my belly button? And a bunch of schoolgirls and their snotty parents isn't the world.'

Mr Jack stirs. 'That's beside the point. How did you get this picture, Cyril?'

'I got a phone call this morning from Norm Thompson at the *Herald*. It turned up on the desk of some Fashion Editor. She thought he'd like to see it, thank God he was bright enough to see the implications and ring me.'

'Who else, do you suppose?'

'Probably every newspaper in the country.'

'You can stop it.'

'I've tried that, already. I've spent the entire day on the telephone, toll calls all over the country, the Press Association, every magazine, every advertising agency I can think of. I've pleaded with editors, bullied them that the picture is under embargo, threatened them with legal action if they use it.'

'So what's the problem?' I say, cheekily.

'The problem is, Alex, that this picture has brought the swimming association into disrepute and you may no longer be an amateur.'

'Even if it never gets used anywhere?'

'I believe that may be so. I shall have to consult my fellow members of the executive committee. It will mean an expensive special meeting.'

'Even if,' asks Mr Jack suddenly, 'it could be shown there was malicious intent, that Alex has been the victim of some scheme to discredit her.'

'I can't believe that. And the fact remains, she was there, in those ... immodest and revealing scraps, parading round in front of a large sign, blatant advertising. See for yourself.'

Out of focus it may be, but the name is legible. It is filtering through that Mr Jack is treading the same path of suspicion as me. So I've nothing to lose, now.

'I've been set up,' I shout. 'I know who it was and I know why. You never wanted me in the team, and she's been trying for years . . .'

'I will not stand for such . . .'

'Perhaps the two of you, in cahoots . . .'

'Alex!' It is Mr Jack, a squat figure of fear and fury standing before me. 'I see your father waiting out in the office. You'll go home and you'll watch your step.'

'I always knew . . .' I say, defeated.

'If you persist, Alex,' says Mr Jack, implacably, 'it will be your loss.'

'What have I left?'

'You've got a lot of friends, Norm Thompson for one. If it wasn't for him, that picture would be all over this morning's *Herald*. You've got to trust them to get you out of this, again.'

He means my 'friend' Mr Upjohn, standing there with a face set in concrete, holding that photograph. It's bitter medicine.

I can't look Maggie in the face next morning at training, let alone her mother, although she makes an effort to be friendly. Naturally, if she thinks her plan has worked. I tell Maggie I'd rather train separately. The water feels like glue; Mr Jack looks as though he's been there all night.

Mercifully, the picture is not in the *Herald* when we get home. I go to school, I go training again in the evening. I go for a fitting for my uniform. Various documents from the Olympic association arrive in the mail. I fend off questions from Keith and Julia, both well-meaning, trying to share how I must be feeling about this fantastic trip coming up, only a week now, golly.

This goes on for five days. Mr Jack keeps telling me to *hold on*.

'It's going to be all right.'

'What are they *doing*?' I keep asking.

'Taking legal advice, I don't know. Going through the proper channels. It's out of my control now, Alex. Sorry, but it is. I've got you out of scrapes before, but this one's gone beyond me.'

'It's inhuman. Why doesn't Mr Upjohn ring, tell me what's going on? I always knew he'd get me in the end,' I say with every bitter bone in my body. One night I line up for my fifth hundred metre time trial and something breaks inside me. I just stand on the side of the pool and weep for my foolishness and vanity, the stupid desire to prove that I was as feminine as the next female through something as basically meaningless and trivial as a school fashion show.

---

Two days before the team is due to assemble in Auckland, Maggie has a bad cold and another stomach-ache. This time it's bad enough to be checked out with blood tests, but they can't find anything, and after a good sleep it goes. Though I still can't look her in the eye, I hear the edge of panic in her voice. They think it's just tension, nerves.

I get a ring from Mr Upjohn.

It's not bad news, but not good news either. It appears that efforts have been made. The photographer has been tracked down; he was engaged by someone ringing on behalf of the school, no one quite knows who, and he was asked not to use a flash because there'd be plenty of light and teenage girls were a little sensitive about having their pictures taken! He was asked to forward the picture to selected papers; no paper, as far as he knows, has used it. All paths lead back to that foolish woman who was simply carried away with trying to raise money for the Crippled Children, but she's so upset and confused they can get little sense out of her. The shop which supplied the bathing-suits said it was her idea. The committee have accepted Mr Jack's assurance that I received no money, and that I was there for simple and worthy motives like wanting to help a charity.

If it was Mrs Benton, I think she must be sweating blood, waiting to see if her little plan is going to work. I'm surprised by the reasonable tone of Mr Upjohn's voice as he goes on to tell me that he believes there may have been some unfortunate dealings behind all this; nevertheless, they are having to take legal advice through the Olympic association in Europe. It may not be through until after we go.

'I'm sorry, Alex,' he says, amazingly. 'It's the best I can do. Obviously, you still have to travel, at this stage. I've been holding the Press at arm's length by threat of legal action, and saying absolutely nothing. I strongly advise you to do the same.'

Oh, don't worry, I assure him, I've been doing that all week. Except, I don't say, for Norm Thompson who comes down to training and has a long chat with Mr Jack, and I'm able to thank him for his help.

I honestly think that Mrs Benton is poised for the kill. If she can get one single newspaper to publish that picture and say underneath that I am wearing a bathing-suit by Rose Marie, I'm out. With her contacts, her money, her slimy husband, it shouldn't be too hard. I don't doubt she's trying, even as the days tick by. But the next day, she's got more important things to worry about than her obsession with Alex Archer, or even going to Rome for the Olympic Games.

---

I didn't find out until late next morning when Mr Upjohn appears at our front door, looking as though someone has pricked his chest with a pin. He's wearing a thick polo-neck jumper round his bullish neck. I believe he has come to tell me that I'm out of the team.

'Mrs Archer, can I come in?' he says with overbearing politeness. This is not the voice of my executioner, I think. It's the voice of someone who is seeing his little Olympic team falling apart at the seams. He waits until we're all sitting.

'Alex, I'm sorry to have to tell you, Maggie's ...'

Maggie? I grip my knees hard and challenge him with my eyes to get it over with. I've had one of these messages before.

'She's what?'

'In hospital. Early this morning, emergency surgery for acute peritonitis. I'm afraid she's on the critical list.'

'Oh, dear God,' says Mum beside me. 'Oh, no.'

'Her father rang me this morning. It appears she's had these pains ...'

'I know.'

They both look at me. 'You knew? Why didn't you say anything?' he says.

The unfairness of this makes me angry. 'How could I? I'm not Maggie's mother or sister or anything. She kept telling me it was OK, just a little pain, gripes, constipation, tension, nerves, nothing an aspirin or a laxative wouldn't fix.'

'Oh, God,' says Mum the nurse. 'The worst thing.'

'What's peritonitis?' I say.

'Inflamation throughout the peritoneal cavity sometimes due to a burst appendix, very dangerous,' says Mum. 'How long, the pain?'

'When she came back from Aussie. Said it'd started over there, came and went.' Looking back, I realize she was terrified to admit it was anything brewing. So, I dare say, was her mother.

What am I feeling? Relief that I'm still going, agony for her that she's not, guilt that I didn't bully her into going to a doctor; but then she did, and they didn't find anything; anger with her mother for not taking her seriously.

'Her father rang me this morning. Of course Rome is out. They've been with her all night.'

'Can I go and see her? Where is she?'

'A private hospital in Epsom. I doubt you'll be allowed. And the team assembles tomorrow.'

'Perhaps you'll have another bit of bad news before then, Mr Upjohn.' He actually looks hangdog. Mum stiffens, and looks puzzled.

'It's nothing Mum.'

I don't even want to go to Rome now. You can't have a team of one. Maggie, you can't die on me. You can't.

The hospital, a two-storey building among some lovely trees, is not all that far away from our house, so after he's gone, I announce I'm riding over to see Maggie, whatever he might say. There's only one way to find out if I can see her, and that's to go there. Mum offers a lift, because there's a freezing cold wind blowing, but I'd rather go alone. I pick the occasional pink blossom from trees along the way. In the car-park outside is the black Super Snipe I know so well.

The nurse at the reception desk does not look up when I approach the desk. The message is clear, children wait till I've finished. So I wait. I'll wait, madam, all day and all night if necessary.

'Can I see Maggie Benton, please?'

She looks up and her eyes narrow. 'I'm sorry. She's not allowed visitors except family.'

'I'm family. A close cousin. I've just arrived from Whangarei.'

She looks me up and down suspiciously and I pray that she has not seen me on my bicycle through the glass doors. 'If you wait, I'll check with the sister.'

'I'll wait.' She dials a number and mutters into the phone. 'I'm sorry, Miss ...?' I murmur Benton. 'Maggie is not allowed visitors, and won't be allowed any for several days.'

'Her parents are here?'

'I believe so.'

'Good. Then I'll find them.' I head off down the nearest corridor, blindly, dropping petals off my little bunch of blossoms.

'Miss Benton! You can't see her. You're not allowed ...' Try to stop me, you old crow, I think grimly.

I've walked down several corridors between buildings, trying to look as though I'm on some sort of official message, before I know I'm hopelessly lost. Most of the doors are forbiddingly closed; there's that hospital smell, musk and disinfectant in the central heating. There's no sign of a door marked Miss M. Benton, or her parents keeping their vigil in a corridor. Then I see a youngish nurse with a friendly face, and several red stripes on her white uniform.

'Please. Can you help me?'

'Maybe.' Scottish too, I note.

'I'm ... I just need to see Maggie Benton, please.'

She looks at me hard, and I see a flicker of recognition, which is not all that surprising for people with good memories. 'I know you. You're off to Rome tomorrow, aren't you?'

'Day after. Oh please, tell me ...'

'I'm sorry ... you obviously know she was admitted last night and why. She's in some danger.'

'You mean she could die?'

She doesn't answer directly, which in some ways is worse than an empty reassurance. I suppose I hadn't really believed Mr Upjohn.

'It could be several days before we know. I'm sorry, Alex. I've read about you two in the papers.'

'How's she feeling, does she know, that her trip ...?'

'I think so, poor lass. She's pretty groggy, sleeping mostly, will be for days. There's a nurse with her all the time.'

'If she's sleeping, can I see her, just see her, stand in the doorway?'

She hesitates. 'I suppose so.'

'Is her mother in there?'

'She's not left since she came down from theatre. I imagine Mrs Benton would be glad to see you. People need support, at times like this.'

You imagine wrong, I think, following the white uniform, white shoes squeaking on the polished floor.

She gently pushes on a door which says 'No Visitors' and I see a hospital bed, a shape, tubes, drips, bottles of blood hanging upside down. A sleeping face which I can barely recognize, as white as the pillow case it is lying on. Two arms outside the covers tethered by tubes with blood and some colourless liquid running in, or out. A nurse standing at the washbasin behind the door, doing something that nurses do. A nice room, not awful, hospital green but shades of yellow, with carpets, pictures, flowers, bedside cupboard. And Mrs Benton sitting, notably upright.

'Mrs Benton?' says the nurse in a low voice. 'Alex just wanted to see her.'

She turns. I'm glad the Scottish nurse has shut the door and moved on. After a long blank stare, Mrs Benton turns her back on me. I've seen mothers like this before, too: pale and staring with big grey circles of fatigue under their unseeing eyes; hair flat and uncombed; determined not to crack. Beyond sleep.

'I just wanted to give her these,' I whisper, waving my tatty little bunch of blossoms in the air. 'What can I say, the trip won't be the same. Get better quickly. I'm sorry.'

She gets up deliberately and comes over. I'm being shown the door, shown out.

'Didn't you read the sign, No Visitors.'

'The nurse said ...'

'No Visitors. Maggie is desperately ill and you come crashing in, even here, Maggie at death's door, will I never get any peace from you?'

'She's not going to die.'

'It's fifty-fifty.'

'She's not going to die,' I whisper fiercely. 'She's not going to Rome, but she's not going to die.'

'That's what you wanted all along, isn't it. All the kudos, the glory. You didn't want to share it with Maggie.'

I am speechless. I can only look at the ceiling as two nurses squeak along the corridor outside.

'I think I'd better go,' I say.

'Please do.'

I'm looking at my big feet, feeling very large and far too healthy in my jeans and face flushed from riding while Maggie lies over there. There is just one thing I have to say.

'That day, the fashion parade. I didn't believe her when she told me she had a bad pain, why she went home. I thought it was some other reason.'

There is a long silence. 'Why are you telling me this? Alex?'

'I feel bad about it. I'd hate it if she thought I hadn't believed her. Maggie's one of the straightest people I know. I just want to put the record straight.'

Her face doesn't flicker. I open the door.

'I'll come again tomorrow, before the team meeting. I want to say goodbye.' I realize you could take that statement two ways. Her silence as she sits slowly down beside the bed confirms all my suspicions. She won't object to me calling again. She owes me that much.

---

I have dreamed for years of this day. Training for the last time in that repulsive water, going to school just to say goodbye to my class and the teachers, enduring Three Cheers for Alex at assembly. Finishing my packing, telling Gran yet again that of course all the things she's made for me are just wonderful. Collecting my schedules from Mr Jack, ringing Keith and Julia and a few others to say goodbye. Tonight is the first full team meeting, seeing all the others who have trained at their sports for five or ten or fifteen years.

All I want to do is weep. It's all such a mess. It wasn't supposed to be like this. I feel stale and exhausted and anything but fit at training. School is a nightmare. I should be gloriously fit and on top of the world. I keep seeing Maggie lying there gaunt and white as a corpse, and hearing the humiliating judgement of some lawyer in Rome or Switzerland or somewhere deciding I'm for the chop.

Mum rings the hospital, because one of her old nursing mates works there, and finds out that Maggie is holding on, but only just. She's not making the improvement expected for someone who's an athelete, super fit; the heavy cold when she had the operation isn't helping. And when I go to see her, Mum comes with me, and stands quietly in the doorway while I go over to the bed and gently kiss Maggie's damp white forehead. Mrs Benton has sunk into the chair. She doesn't even look up.

The team meeting passes in a dream. There are all these men and only six women, and I'm the youngest by about ten years. Oh, Maggie. The manager talks of tickets, passports, vaccination certificates, and the thirty-seven pounds of personal baggage we are allowed, and seven pounds of sports equipment — what does a pair of racing togs weigh, three ounces? Tomorrow's plans. I can't take anything more in.

### Monday, August 8.

Totally exhausted. No training. Mr Jack says I'll need all my strength for the trip tomorrow. Today was frantic. Medical examination. Collect uniforms, put them on for 'Meet the Press'. Norm Thompson has a big story about Maggie in this morning's paper. Maggie Benton ill, 15-year-old Swimmer Misses Out On Rome Trip. He tells me he's just rung the hospital again, no change. So also does Mr Upjohn, quite subdued. I like my chaperon, Mrs Churchill, she's cuddly. *My* chaperon. I get weepy again over my cup of tea. I'm the Water Baby of the team, some baby! When the team photo is taken in the Domain wintergardens, all the women have to stand together behind the managers. I'm the tallest, so I go in the middle. We have these *terrible* red hats and plastic granny handbags.

After lunch, the Civic Farewell at the Town Hall with Mr Robinson swallowed up by his mayoral furs, and some old men droning on for ages. We are the biggest team ever sent north of the Equator, costing £34,000. Wow. Mum and Dad take me to the team hotel. Tomorrow morning we'll be up at six, because the plane goes at nine-thirty from Whenuapai. They are coming out to see me off. I don't think I'll sleep tonight. Maggie is the same.

### Saturday, August 13.

Somewhere, an hour out of Singapore.

Sorry diary, it's all been a bit much. These are just notes until I can concentrate a bit better. Let's see — late leaving Auckland, mechanical fault to plane, grey and raining as per usual, couple of hundred people to see us off. Entire family, Keith *and* his Mum, Mr Jack and Mrs Jack, Julia, all weeping and waving. Oddly, the Richmonds, who I feel guilty about not visiting. She's older. I remember Keith
telling me about the fights, Andy and his old man. Today, he's smoking a pipe and genial. Most odd, *Mr* Harold Benton, smooth as silk in a suit, kissing me goodbye. Maggie is holding on Oh, and that young reporter, Grant Davies, ticked pink because he's going to start work at the *Herald* next week. He was offered a job, quite a step up from a small-town paper. Says he's now a shorthand speed fiend!

Seedney — saw the bridge and city centre and Botany Bay from plane, not much else. After that, red sand and desert for *hours* to Darwin (hot), sea and islands to Singapore. They let me go up in the cockpit as we approached Singapore. The ships! Being the baby has some advantages.

Singapore was full of surprises. Started badly, after a fifteen hour flight, twenty hours without sleep: a mix-up, no bus to take us to hotel, long hot wait. You can't imagine what tropical heat is like until you're in it.

Raffles Hotel, fantastic. Green, shady, cane chairs to sit in. But a visitor there for me! I hoped it might be someone from the High Commission, with news of Maggie but it turned out to be some friend of the Bentons, yes, Joyce Benton who used to live in Singapore, their daughter Maggie. Mrs Benton had rung her last night! No change to Maggie. The woman was slim and smart, just what you might expect of a Benton buddy. I thanked her, said I was sorry, thinking that was all, *but* she floored me completely by saying that Mrs Benton had asked if she would take me away, let me sleep in a decent bed, show me the sights, take me training at Singapore Swimming Club, Maggie's old haunt. I just stood and gaped. Mrs Churchill was happy to let me go; gave her two days off looking after me. It was a wonderful two days. Swam a bit at the club, which is vast, but too hot and too full of people for anything serious. Visited Tiger Balm Gardens, saw amazing street scenes, beggars, rickshaws, laundry on poles out of windows, went to a fantastical Chinese restaurant and had to learn to use chopsticks in a great hurry at a restaurant so swanky that I wondered what I was doing there. This lady, whose name was Josephine, had a lovely house in green jungly gardens, amahs and gardeners, a husband who worked in a shipping company. *And*, imagine this, she'd known Mrs Benton at school in England. Seems Mrs Benton was *very* bright, but her father was a mean old Sir somebody, huge great house, servants, antiques, and no money; didn't believe in educating women. Wouldn't let her finish university, had to come home and look after her cranky old Dad. Then she drove ambulances in the war and got married and moved to Singapore. Classic case of wasted talent, which turned out to be the Classics, Latin and Greek! Great shame, she's a marvellous organizer, said Josephine, but Harold's, well, you know, very demanding, and treats her like a child. No wonder she wanted so badly to go to Rome. I'm glad I know this. Anyway, the rest of the team went berserk buying cameras and watches and radios in Change Alley. Josephine took me shopping for a camera too — a Zeiss, with money from Mr Jack. She bargained beautifully. We put a call through to the Bentons just before going to the airport — got Mr Benton. Maggie's not yet out of danger because that cold she had last week has brought on chest complications, which are causing concern, a sort of pneumonia, he said. I sent all my love, thinking of you, Maggie. Boy, is it hot here! We had to get out of the plane in our uniforms, stockings, blazers and all, which stuck to us with sweat. The child beggars upset me terribly, dirty, some mutilated, amputated. And the dirt.

### Sunday, August 14.

Darkness. Somewhere over India. Can't sleep. My watch says

two a.m. but that's nonsense, 'cause we took off from Calcutta at three a.m. after sitting in the plane for two hours while they refuelled. Temperature was 110 Fahrenheit inside the plane. If this is what it's like at night, daytime must be hell on earth. Got a cup of water and a towel and kept my forehead and arms wet, what else could you do? We are all looking very hangdog. Mrs Churchill's feet have swollen something terrible, some of the athletes' too, can't get their shoes on. The men are unshaven and smelly. There's a red streak outside, dawn somewhere. Karachi soon. Another sweltering place. We can get out of the plane here, they say. I can't wait ... Oh yes, one of the crew came back earlier and told us the All Blacks had drawn the Third Test in South Africa, so they lost the first and won the second and I'm glad they are not having it all their own way ...

I stopped writing. Something was bothering me. It crossed my mind that people sometimes say they have known when someone's died, from thousands of miles away. I think myself back to Maggie's little yellow room, the Scottish nurse, and poor sad Mrs Benton sitting there for the past five days with those terrible plastic tubes of blood. Please Maggie, if it's you, hold on, hold *on*. I closed my eyes, and said the nearest thing to a prayer I knew, and drifted off to sleep. The hostess, God bless her, didn't try too hard to wake me for breakfast, because she knew a sleep of exhaustion when she saw it, and it was only three hours since we had dinner in the middle of the night!

I woke to a change of engine noise, and my ears popping, and needed a pee. Both toilets were full, so I looked idly out the window on to a seaside city below, as brown and dry and dusty looking as Singapore was green. The hostess was busy tidying things up in the galley nearby. I grinned at her. What I got in reply was not the cheerful grin she's had since Singapore. Despite the chic uniform and smart make-up, she was not that much older than me, and she spoke with a broad Aussie accent.

'Do you get off here?' I said.

'I hope so,' she snapped, dropping something, slamming shut a cupboard.

I peered out the window again. 'I've seen that bit of the city before, a few minutes ago,' I said.

'I doubt it. The whole place looks the same. Dry as dust.'

'I suppose, sometimes you have to wait, go around again to wait your turn, or if you have a problem.'

'How ...?' The quick glance out the window gave her away. We both looked. Though we were fairly low, there was no sign of the landing-gear.

'Don't worry. Go back to your seat. Quickly.'

'But I need ...'

'You'll have to wait.' She rapped on the toilet doors. 'Please return to your seats.' And to me, *sotto voce*. 'Don't say anything, please.'

I could try my prayers, I thought, as I swung myself upwards towards my seat and climbed over Mrs Churchill. The plane was climbing again. Out the window I could see a green patch of sports field, a mosque, flat tops of buildings, streets, dry exhausted trees; then the airport and trucks driving round which we later found out were crash wagons with firemen and extinguishers.

Then the crew began to tear up the carpet in the aisle just ahead of us and fiddle round with bits of machinery thus revealed. Mrs Churchill turned to look at me.

'What's going on?'

'I think the landing-gear has stuck,' I said, and though it was stuffy, she deliberately got out her blanket and hid herself right under it.

Well, I thought, if it's curtains, they may find my last will and testament amidst the rubble and bits of flesh, so I got out Gran's My Trip Book and found a fresh page.

It wasn't Maggie about to die, it was me.

Years and years of expensively trained athletes, and the kindly granny from Christchurch hiding her head beside me, about to evaporate in a puff of smoke on a Karachi desert. I began to write, fast.

> There's a problem with the undercarriage, and it looks as though we might have to land on our belly, or go circling round the earth for ever. The crew hasn't actually told us yet, but they are scrabbling around on all fours in the aisle, doing something fairly vital from the looks on their faces. I know because I'm too jolly smart for my own good, and the

air hostess isn't smart enough yet to lie convincingly. So this is the last Will and Testament of the would-be lawyer, the one in four in the classroom who didn't quite make it to adulthood, Alexandra Beatrice Archer, aged 15 and nine months, being of sound mind and very sound body, but right at this moment very unsound indeed, wobbly in the pit of my stomach, and my bladder. I haven't got much to leave except the stuff in my bedroom and the kids are welcome to that *if* they can share it out without fighting. I'd like Julia to have my bike 'cause hers isn't all that marvellous, and Andy's transistor radio to go to Keith. If you find the drop pearl necklace I'm wearing now, can you bury it with whatever you find of me, please. At sea, I think, yes, sprinkle me somewhere near Rangitoto because of Andy and what he may or may not have done in the navy and because he was happiest sailing his boat.

And Maggie, old friend? I wonder where we'll meet again. Somewhere un-earthly very shortly or somewhere earthly in September, if you've won your battle and I've won mine. It's been fun, hasn't it, mostly. Thanks for a good fight. If you make it and I don't, keep at it — there's the Commonwealth Games in '62 and they think it might be Tokyo in '64. Good luck, my friend. The plane has gone very quiet, because it's fairly obvious there's a spot of bother. Mum and Dad, thank you for everything, doing everything you did to get me here, all the love and support that went with it. Perhaps once you've got over it, life without me will be easier, three normal children without that large girl rampaging around causing so much *trouble*. Gran, too, I know you worked yourself to the bone, burning the midnight oil, all those lovely clothes in my suitcase, such a damn shame. Wherever I'm going, I know that Andy will be there. He didn't tell me anything about an air crash, perhaps he thought it better not to, but nothing's as simple as that, is it? He said I was going to Rome, not that I'd get there. Who'd have thought that Maggie and I would come to this — her missing the trip and quite possibly dead, even as I write this if my intuitions were correct, or me maybe about to be snuffed out. I'm feeling surprisingly calm. I'd like to have played Joan. I'd like to have had a child. I'd like to have stood in a courtroom and fought for someone.

Mrs Churchill is a hump of quivering blanket beside me,

> poor thing ... the crew are still active ... I've just looked
> out the window, and Glory Be to God, the wheels are sl-ow-
> ly appearing. There's a lot of activity on the tarmac as I see
> it for the last time, and we straighten up for the approach.
> The crew are running back to strap themselves into their
> seats ...

My heart was going gi-donk gi-donk again, 200 per minute as we came in to land, over yellow water, rivers, scrubby grass, mud-coloured villages, skinny tropical trees. We straightened up, came ever lower, touched, bounced, touched again, screeched, roared, bounced ... but it was all right, the plane was level and slowing and the crash wagons were converging on us, and a few people began to clap somewhere at the back. We have landed, gloriously, normally. Did I imagine the whole thing? Mrs Churchill has poked her head up. I should have gone to the toilet because the relief was so enormous that I knew I now must, or wet my pants. I undid my seat belt and climbed over Mrs Churchill and dashed, against all the rules, while the plane was still moving fast, past the hostess strapped to her seat, and into the toilet. I didn't know which to do first, sit on it, spew into it, but it was so small I could actually do both at once, into the basin.

By the time I had calmed down and splashed water all over my face and arms, the plane was moving quite slowly. The hostess was busy again, preparing to open the door, let the heat in. She managed a wan smile.

'The hydraulics went,' she murmured. 'They wound the jolly thing down by hand. You wouldn't read about it, would you?'

'You would in the newspapers. I've just written my will.'

'You can tear it up.'

---

We were ten hours on the ground in Karachi, while they fixed the plane. I couldn't bring myself to write my diary; I remember very little of being taken to a hotel to have a sleep in cool bedrooms, on white sheets, or of taking off again. Landing in Cairo and long waits in the airport lounge there; taking off again and flying at last over the Mediterranean which was every bit as blue as I'd been told.

The last leg, over rocky Sicily and the toe of Italy. Getting ready to step out at Rome airport; uniforms and trying to push swollen feet into stiff shoes. Out the window I can see villages, churches and cyprus trees: Praise Be, the Seven Hills of the city, the Colosseum, the Tiber itself. Someone thinks they are seeing the Olympic stadium, by the river. I look back down the plane. Everyone is craning against their seatbelts to see something out the windows. We've worked for this.

The landing, taxiing, breathing for the first time — pure Roman sunshine, clear and hot. There is a band to meet us, dark Roman men, playing something I recognize, the trumpet tune, the triumphal march from *Aida*! Everyone looks so tanned here — we are winter white, pallid. We don't look like a bunch of athletes and my knees for one are trembling as I walk down the steps to touch Roman ground.

A strange flat bus takes us to the terminal. All the signs are in Italian! There are banners and posters everywhere with the five circles of the Olympic emblem. Customs, passports, tickets, painfully sore feet in our too-tight shoes, swelteringly hot in our black woollen blazers.

But proud, oh yes, *proud*: I come from New Zealand, that's way over the other side of the globe. We have taken six exhausting days to get here, travelled longer and further than any other team. It has cost our country £34,000 to send us. We have earned our right to be here, each one of us. You can see New Zealand on our pockets, and the silver fern which is our national emblem, because ours is a very green country with bush and mountains and rivers, about the same size as Italy, but more spectacular, wilder, newer.

And these tears I'm crying are because I am here, I'm at the end of my tether and I still have a heavy weight at the bottom of my stomach. Maggie may be dead for all I know. I may never swim here, for all I know.

We are standing round as we've done in all the airports, waiting like sheep to be herded, but here, it is different. There are Press photographers and reporters because we are rather special guests, and I seem to get more than my fair share of attention, though

I'm past caring what I look like.

'Bella!' one of the photographers whispers as he looks down into his Rollei. 'Benvenuto!' 'Grazie,' I say.

There's a reception committee too, well-dressed men in lightweight suits, who turn out to be from our embassy here. I wouldn't have taken much notice of them, as they seem to be talking about serious matters to the managers, Mr Upjohn and people — except that I see him pointing me out and one heads my way.

'Alex Archer?'

'Yes.'

'I'm Colin Browning, attaché at the embassy here.' He is fair and almost too smooth, but wearing a little New Zealand silver kiwi pin on his lapel, one of us.

'Welcome to Rome. I hope you are not too exhausted.'

'Fairly,' I say.

'I've two messages for you, which I was told to make sure you got the minute you landed.'

Maggie has died. But he's smiling, he doesn't look like the bearer of bad tidings. Maggie is OK, but I'm out.

'A Mr Harold Benton was in touch with our office yesterday. The message is that your friend Maggie is fine, she's over the worst and doing well, going home from hospital in two or three days.'

Oh, Maggie. I just stand there. A week's real tears well up and overflow. He takes me gently by the elbow towards a seat by the window. Outside all sorts of big jets are parked — B.O.A.C., Qantas, Alitalia, Pan American, Lufthansa, Air France. Funny how you notice these things when you're steamed up.

Mr Upjohn comes over and sits down beside me, which I don't find especially comforting.

'That's good news to hear, Alex, isn't it?' he says. 'The other is equally good. Mr Browning tells me that the games association has cabled. You've been cleared. The circumstances were sufficiently cloudy. It will go no further.'

'I can swim?'

'You can swim.'

I fumble for a hanky, but Mr Upjohn anticipates me and hands me one. I see something in his eyes, respect maybe, which makes me feel that I don't need to keep avoiding him as I've done since we left; that I'm not alone with poor flustered Mrs Churchill in this strange place. I have in fact two people, stand-in parents, to look after me. His smile is not the smile of a crocodile any more.

'Well, team of one,' he says. 'I think we should get you some sleep.'

'It's the middle of the day,' I say. 'I'd rather go for a swim. Can I go to the Olympic pool?'

'Why not?' he says, and stands. 'We appreciate your help, Colin. It looks like they're moving out to the bus now.'

Lead on, I say. *Arrivederci Roma* is being played on the sound system. Arrivederci Andy, and Maggie-getting-better, and all my family still having winter over the other side of the globe. Until we meet again, I'll be giving it my best shot.

Through the swing doors, out of the terminal into the Roman sunshine, full of flowers and trees and young people wearing the clothes of summer and freedom and song.

To the Olympic village and the pool and whatever times I can pull out of my hat against girls who have had a summer's training, a summer's racing. The opening ceremony and meeting Dawn Fraser and seeing the Sistine Chapel and *Aida*.

*Andiamo.* Let's go!